Halsey's Pride

Halsey's Pride

LYNN HALL

CHARLES SCRIBNER'S SONS
NEW YORK

Charles Scribner's Sons Books for Young Readers
Macmillan Publishing Company
866 Third Avenue, New York, NY 10022
Collier Macmillan Canada, Inc.

Printed in the United States of America
10 9 8 7 6 5 4 3 2

Library of Congress Cataloging-in-Publication Data
Hall, Lynn.
Halsey's pride / Lynn Hall. / 1st ed.   p.   cm.
Summary: Thirteen-year-old March, an epileptic, comes to live with her dog breeder father and through her growing attachment to her father's prize dog, Pride, learns a great deal about love, truth, courage and how to cope with adverse fate.
[1. Epilepsy—Fiction.   2. Dogs—Fiction.
3. Fathers and daughters—Fiction.]   I. Title.
PZ7.H1458Han   1990   [Fic]—dc20 89–34998 CIP AC
ISBN 0–684–19155–5

Halsey's Pride

One

Summer twilight; blue haze over grass and trees; the rasp of insect song.

There was activity in the flat green field and noise from human voices, from the pounding of tent stakes, the muffled roar of generators from motor homes, and the barking of dogs. But in this quiet corner of the fairground the insect song dominated.

It was a small county fairground in southern Illinois, and the pounding and preparations were for the local kennel club's annual dog show. Although the show wouldn't begin until nine the next morning, already the parking area was filling with trailers, motor homes, and vans.

Long trucks marked Roy Jones Dog Shows had arrived from Indiana and were being relieved of their loads of ring fencing and other equipment. Half a dozen of the Jones crew were erecting a striped tent three hundred feet long, while others paced and measured off the eighteen show rings and stopped to visit with exhibitors.

In the quiet area near the open-sided livestock buildings, where the insect song was still the prevalent sound, two rigs had parked close enough for friendliness, distant enough for privacy. One was a small, battered trailer hitched to a station wagon. The other was a middle-aged Winnebago motor home whose tires showed many thousands of miles of wear. The motor home had just pulled in, and no one had yet emerged.

"Looks like March Goodman's rig," Dick Peterson said to his wife. He and Diane sat outside their trailer and van in folding chaise longues, their limbs weighted with laziness. In front of them, a small portable hibachi still held glowing coals and gave off the lingering fragrance of steaks and buttered baked potatoes sealed in aluminum foil.

Just to the left of their reclining chairs stood a folding exercise pen six feet square. Within the pen two collies lay watching and dozing, a young sable bitch who was entered for the next day's judging, and a gray-muzzled senior citizen who always got to come along for the ride.

"That's not the Goodmans'," Diane argued. "Their motor home is a lighter color, with blue stripes."

"Bet you a beer."

"You're on."

They were a pleasant young couple, rather beefy and hearty and well matched. In anticipation of winning their bet, they both turned to watch the door of the motor home.

In a few minutes the door did open, and three people emerged: an elderly man with extremely stooped shoulders, an energetic, squarely built woman in her mid-forties, and a very large man who looked as soft and pale as an ice-cream sundae.

"You owe me a beer," Dick murmured to his wife. Without moving from her chair Diane opened the cooler beside her, fished inside it, and tossed a cold, wet can into her husband's lap.

"Hi, March, Dan," she called.

Dick added, "Need any help setting up?"

"Nah, thanks, we've got our system down pat," the woman called back.

The large man began pulling wire exercise pens from a storage space under the motor home and setting them up in a row before the Winnebago. The woman brought dogs out and shuttled them into the pens as fast as the pens went up, collies and tervurens, a bearded collie, a pair of giant schnauzers, and one small corgi.

The old man wandered close to the Petersons' pen and leaned over to stroke the head of the old collie, who rose to crowd out the younger dog for the stranger's attention.

"That's a good head, for a dog that old," the man offered. "Ain't hardly coarsened at all, has it? I'd bet you there's some Halsey's Pride back in that old boy's pedigree. Is there?"

Dick and Diane looked at each other. Dick said, "Halsey's Pride? I don't think so. That doesn't ring a bell. He's mostly Parader and Brandwyn breeding. I don't remember any dog named Halsey's Pride in his pedigree."

The old man stiffened and glared at Dick. "You ain't been in collies very long then, have you? Never heard of

3

Halsey's Pride. I bet you never heard of me then, either. Huh? Never heard of Clinton Halsey?"

Dick and Diane exchanged a lightning look. Diane, who was the better liar of the two, said quickly, "Well, of course we've heard of Clinton Halsey. What collie breeder hasn't heard of Clinton Halsey?" She shot a "help" message to Dick with her eyes.

"How about a beer?" Dick said.

The old man sank to a perch on the end of Diane's chaise, just missing her feet. He accepted the cold can Dick handed him, but he set it in the grass and used both hands to work a wallet from his back pocket. Gnarled fingers trembled as they brought from the wallet a small and much-worn photograph.

"There. That's him. That's the great Halsey's Pride. Best in Show winner. One of the greatest foundation sires in the breed."

Diane bent and squinted over the photograph, which was so small and faded that no details of the dog were discernible beyond the general outline of a collie with a broad white shawl-collar marking around his neck.

"Gorgeous," she said politely, and passed the photo over to Dick.

"So that's the famous . . ." Dick floundered.

"Halsey's Pride," Diane rescued him. "Tell us about him. You bred him yourself, did you?"

The old man tucked the photo and the wallet away, opened the beer can, and took a long, throat-bobbing pull. When the can came down, Halsey's long weathered face had a light, almost radiant expression.

4

"That was a great dog. I knew it from the minute he was whelped. I picked up that little wet newborn pup and I said to myself, 'This is a great one.' And I was right. There wasn't a judge in the world that could ever say no to that animal. We'd sail into a show ring and it was just like the other dogs weren't even there. All the way to Best in Show."

"How many Best in Shows did he win?" Diane asked.

"Just the one, and then I retired him. Best in Show is as high as you can go. No point in showing him after that, was there? And besides, I needed him at home for breeding. He was the most sought-after collie stud in the country back then. People shipped bitches to him from all over. New York, California, Japan even. Everybody knew he was a great dog. You young people nowadays, you think you know something about collies. You don't. You never even heard of Pride. I'd be ashamed of my ignorance, if I was you."

Dick and Diane flashed glances again, but Diane kept a straight face and said, "What ever happened to Pride?"

Halsey's face softened again and took on the diffused glow of memory. "He was my constant companion till the day he died at the age of eighteen. I was so broke up, I just couldn't go on breeding after that. I sold out and retired. Once you've bred a perfect dog, where can you go from there, right? You can't do no better than perfect, and I'd already had my perfect dog."

"You must have loved him a lot," Diane said softly, and this time there was no fun in the look she sent her husband.

Halsey's eyes misted. "I never loved nothing that much,

5

before or since. Well, believe I'll walk around a little, stretch the old legs." He stood and began to move away, then hesitated beside the exercise pen and once again stroked the head of the old collie. "That's not a bad one you got here. Not like old Pride, of course, but he ain't a bad one."

When the old man had moved off toward the show rings, Dick and Diane pulled long faces at each other. March and Dan Goodman were within hearing range, feeding the dogs in their pens, so Diane kept her voice low.

"What a nut case. Who do you suppose he is? Somebody's father? He's traveling with the Goodmans, so he must belong to one of them."

They sat in the gathering darkness, too lazy and content to move or to concern themselves with other people's elderly relatives.

"Where'd Dad wander off to?" March asked as she set the last pan of dog food in the last exercise pen. The little corgi dove into the food, wagging her tailless rump.

"Down toward the rings, I think," Dan said. "I feel like a walk, myself. I'll go check out the ring layout for you and keep an eye out for Dad along the way. Want to come?"

March shook her head and nodded toward the dogs in the pens. If she went out of their sight, one or two of the bigger ones would probably jump the flimsy pens and come looking for her. The dogs belonged to clients who paid her fifty dollars a show, per dog, to groom and exhibit, so they represented a major responsibility.

Dan wandered off, pausing for a few minutes beside the Petersons. March watched him with a long, tender look.

6

Hers was a square, plain face roughened by weather and grooved by years of pain and anxiety. But it held also a quality of peace that was rare in her profession.

Leaning against the corner of the motor home in jeans and a faded red T-shirt, March Goodman somehow brought to mind a pioneer matron with skirts blowing against the covered wagon. Her face was that of a stoic, a silent sufferer.

She was placid now as she switched on the motor home's side floodlight and went to work. From each of the twelve pens she retrieved a food dish, washed it, and stored it away. With her long-handled pooper-scooper she raked up chunks of stool from the pens, before the dogs could dirty their coats trampling them, and deposited each chunk in the black plastic bag tied to the side of the motor home.

"Come on over," Diane Peterson called.

March cleaned off the pooper-scooper, set it in its place, and fetched one of the folding chairs stored beneath the motor home. She set it up beside Diane and smiled at both of the Petersons.

They were old friends, the sort of casual friends who gradually emerge from familiar faces to faces with names, over months and years of seeing each other at dog shows. When March won two collie classes and needed someone to take one of her dogs into the ring for the Winners class, Dick Peterson was always quietly available. When the Petersons' bitch needed to be transported to Canada to be bred at a time that coincided with March's annual Canadian dog-show trip, March delivered the bitch and charged nothing.

But it was not yet a personal friendship, not one that extended past the show weekends.

"I see my dad was over here bending your ears," March said as she sank into her chair.

"Telling us about his—"

"His brag dog," March finished wryly.

"Beer? Coke? Seven-Up?" Diane opened the cooler.

"Seven-Up would be nice, thanks."

Dick said, "I believe they've sprayed around here this year. Remember how bad the mosquitoes were last year? I haven't felt a one yet this evening."

Diane handed March the cold green can. "Did your dad really have a Best in Show dog?" She and Dick had been showing collies for seven years now and had only a few championships, half a dozen Best of Breed wins, and one Herding Group fourth place to brag about. To them, Best in Show was beyond even daydreaming about.

"Oh yes," March said wearily, rubbing the can across her forehead, "the Best in Show was real enough. The dog was real enough."

"But?" Diane prompted, sensing a story.

March shrugged and looked away into the distance. Oh yes, the dog was real enough.

"Tell us," Diane urged.

"Oh, you don't want to hear that old stuff. It's a long story. You don't want to get me started on it."

"Sure we do," Dick said. "The TV reception's no good out here, and it's too early to go to bed. We might as well tell stories around the campfire."

March studied their good, familiar faces for a long

8

moment. How much could she tell these two? All of it, probably. What a relief that would be, just to tell somebody about Dad, about Pride, about her own part in it. Just to tell it all.

"Okay, you asked for it. Well, let's see. The Best in Show happened back in 1955, about six months before I went to live with Dad. . . ."

Two

I was thirteen when I went to live with Daddy. Mom and I had been living up north in Champaign with her boyfriend, and I'd spend one month with Daddy every summer.

Life in Champaign hadn't been all that good, but suddenly, now that I was being dumped on Daddy permanently, the old life seemed precious, familiar and precious. I sat back deep in my chair and watched them throw word-knives at each other and wondered how long I'd have to live before the luxury of death would come along.

"So he ran out on you," Daddy said. "I knew he would, Judy. I knew it was just a matter of time."

"He didn't run out on me. We just broke up, and it wasn't my fault." Mom's eyes started to move toward me, but she caught herself in time. "Anyhow, the point is, I'm going to be starting classes next week, and what with going to school full time and working full time and keeping up my grades, I just can't handle . . ."

This time the eyes did get over to me. That was okay. I knew all about it anyhow. She couldn't cope with a thirteen-year-old kid who had foaming-at-the-mouth, falling-down fits. And of course Mike left us, once he got a look at the kid flopping around on the floor, wetting her pants and biting her tongue. What a beautiful sight that must have been. Who could blame him for leaving?

I sighed and looked around the room. Same old room, small and square and dimly lit. The little black-and-white television set against the opposite wall was still on. Daddy had only turned the sound down, as though he hoped we wouldn't interrupt his program too long with our problems.

Cheap brown carpeting covered floorboards that moved when I walked on them. There was a half-high partition between this room and the kitchen. A dead philodendron was taped to its support post.

Near me stood a tall glass-fronted corner cupboard that held Daddy's heart and soul, or might just as well have. It held the ornate silver tray inscribed "Best in Show, Paducah Kennel Club, 1955." Behind it was an array of large blue and purple rosettes, and on the upper shelf were several smaller trophies.

On the wall over my head hung a dozen photographs of Daddy and Pride, standing with various dog-show judges who held rosettes or trophies. Everyone was grinning in those pictures—even the dog, or so it seemed.

I looked at Mom and Daddy and tried to see where I had come from. Mom was narrowly built, with kinky red hair and prominent bones. You could look at her arms and see her as an entire skeleton. She was pretty in a high-strung way. Daddy was thin, too, in his farmer overalls, with dark

11

hair that was disappearing fast from his temples and the back of his head. He had fine brown eyes like mine, but they were set too close together in his narrow head. He looked just like the southern Illinois redneck he was.

I was too square faced and sandy colored to belong to this family. Of course I didn't belong to them. I belonged to myself. They were just stuck with me till I got old enough and well enough to get away from them.

Mom was saying, "I brought you three months' worth of her Dilantin, and she's good about taking it. You don't need to worry about that. The medication pretty much keeps the seizures under control. I'm afraid to let her swim or take tub baths. . . ."

I got up and went out through the kitchen, through the cluttered, smelly laundry porch, and down the back steps into the night air.

It was early September and the twilight was just hitting the blue haze period, when there was full light but no shadows. Beyond the outbuildings was the belt of windbreak pines that sheltered the house from west winds and hid beneath its branches a lifetime's accumulation of farm machinery and household junk. Beyond the trees, barbed-wire fences etched black lines against the hazy blue hay fields. Beyond the hay fields were distant trees, the river, the town, other houses full of other people. But they were safely distant. That was one thing I loved here, the spaces between me and other people.

An ugly gray tiger-striped cat stepped on my feet, leaned against my jeans. I picked him up and carried him with me as I moved slowly toward the dogs.

12

I'd been here in June, when the new kennel building was just poles in the ground and a gradually growing roof. Now it was almost done. It was a long, unpainted plank building with chain-link fencing fanning out on both sides, enclosing long, narrow, graveled runs.

I stopped, surprised at the number of collies flinging themselves at their fences and barking for my attention. The cat poured himself out of my arms and stalked off unnoticed as I started along the row of run gates.

There was Pride in the first run, looking huge and magnificent as he always did. The next four runs held two or three dogs each, and beyond them were pens of puppies, whole litters of puppies in each run.

Just three months ago there had been only Pride, three bitches, and one litter of partially sold pups. Halsey's Kennels was certainly leaping into the collie business.

I went into Pride's run and sat down on his wooden loafing bench. He was all over me, leaping, shoving, wagging, jamming his magnificent long head between my legs, licking at my face. God, it felt good to be welcomed.

He was a tricolored collie, his body a glossy blue-black, his neck and chest and legs and tail tip bright white set off by rich tan penciling on legs and cheeks. Twin tan dots were his eyebrows. I buried my hands deep in his woolly pelt and just loved him.

"You're glad I'm here, anyway, aren't you, Pride? I am, too, just between us two. I don't know how Daddy and I are going to get along together. We never had to for more than a month at a time, you know. He could always put up with me for that short a time. And luckily I never had a seizure

13

in front of him. This is going to be different. I'll have to start school here and everything. I wish I could take you to school with me, huggy-dog. I wish I could take you everywhere with me. I wish you could sleep with me at night and be with me every minute of every day. It would be so much easier with you to hang on to."

He pressed his head against my chest and leaned into me with his whole seventy pounds.

"You don't care if I have epilepsy. You wouldn't even care if I had a seizure right in front of you, would you? No, you wouldn't care; you've got better sense than anybody else I know. You know what?" He lifted his head and cocked it. "When I get old enough and get over my epilepsy, I'm going to go off someplace all alone and just live with dogs. No people. I'll take you with me if you're still alive then, and you can live in the house and sleep on the bed with me and everything. Want to?"

He thrashed his tail.

"March," Mom called.

I sighed and grunted as I struggled to stand. Pride crowded between me and his run gate, to keep me in with him.

Mom and Daddy were waiting at the side of the house, beside her car. She dropped her arms onto my shoulders, her fingers laced behind my hair.

"I have to get started, darlin'. It's a four-hour drive back, and you know how sleepy I get on long drives."

She peered into my face, trying to read something there. Forgiveness for dumping me? I hunched under the weight of her arms and said, "Drink Cokes while you drive. That'll keep you awake. Pull over if you feel real sleepy."

"Listen, Marchie, you do understand about this, don't you?" She glanced at Daddy, who turned and shuffled away, kicking at leaves. "You do understand that I'm doing this for us, for you and me, so when I've got my teaching degree I can take care of both of us without having to depend on anybody else."

"I know."

"And that I'm going to have to give it one hundred percent of my energy and attention, especially at first. It's been years since I did any studying, and frankly I'm kind of scared about it. You know, whether I can keep up with the work."

"I know."

She pulled me to her for a long hug that almost broke down my strength.

"I'm going to miss you, darlin' daughter. You don't know how much I'm going to miss you these next three years. But this really truly is the best place for you to be, for now. And your daddy's going to need your help, what with this big new kennel and everything. You help him all you can, hear? And don't forget your pills and your doctor appointments. You'll be in charge of those now. You're big enough to take care of that for yourself, okay?"

I nodded and made a spasmodic grab for her, locking my arms around her waist. She stiffened for an instant, studied me to see if I was starting a seizure.

"I'm okay," I said quickly.

"Write and let me know how you like your new school," she said, easing out of my hug.

I grinned. "You, too."

With a wave she drove away, out the lane and onto the

gravel road and off in a cloud of dust. I looked at my daddy and he looked at me.

He turned away from me to go back into the house, back to his television program. I felt a sudden desperate need to make contact with him, to know that he was actually looking at me and accepting me into his life.

"Who are all the new bitches?" I asked quickly.

He looked at me then, hesitated, and came back across the grass in my direction. Together we turned and went toward the kennel. Its raw pine flanks were orange on the sunset side, blue on the far side.

"Are you going to paint it white?" I asked, stroking the building as I passed it.

"White or green, I haven't decided."

"I could help paint."

"Yeah, reckon you could."

We passed Pride's run and stopped before the next one. "That lighter bitch in there is Honey. You remember her. The other one is a new one I just got last week. Pandora, her name is. She's a five-year-old, but I got her cheap and she's got good breeding behind her. She's in whelp to Pride already. These three in here are all new," he said, moving down the line. "They come from a commercial breeder in Kansas that was going out of business. Quality ain't much good, but they'll produce for me. These in here I shipped in from Colorado."

Down the line we went. He was speaking happily now, more happily than I'd ever heard him. As he described each brood bitch he stood taller and taller, a rich man counting

16

his treasures. We went full circle around the building and stopped in front of Pride.

Here Daddy said nothing at all. He just looked down at that dog and gloated.

"Pride's going to be busy, with all those wives," I said.

Daddy gazed down into the collie's eyes. "He's the key to the whole thing. Success don't just happen to a person, March. You remember that. You have to see those opportunities while they're so little no one else can see them. And then you do what you have to do to make your own success.

"I've been a dirt-poor forty-acre farmer all my life, girl. I never had nothing I didn't go out and get for myself any way I could. Including your mother. I spent years showing my collies and never winning enough to shine your shoes on. Those other collie people, they'd see old Clint Halsey coming into the ring, and they'd say, 'Good. We don't have to worry about him, he's easy to beat.'

"And then finally my good dog did come along, and I was smart enough to know it. Smart enough to hang onto him and keep showing him till he started getting him some good wins, till he went all the way to the top. And now I'm smart enough to know how to cash in on him. I've bet every penny I've got on buying bitches to breed him to, building this big new kennel. And he's going to pay me back by making me rich. Those pups of his are worth three hundred apiece, five hundred for some of them. And I aim to have a big enough operation to cash in, you understand?"

I nodded. It was a wonderful dream. I began seeing myself as a permanent part of it, breeding and selling beautiful collies right here on the farm for the rest of my life.

17

"Can I go to some shows with you?" I asked.

"Oh, maybe, once in a while. If it don't interfere with school. It'd be more help, though, if you'd stay home and take care of the kennel while I went to the shows."

I looked up at him, but his eyes slid away from mine. Was he thinking about me having one of my fits at a dog show and embarrassing him in front of all his friends? Slowly I let my breath out and looked back toward Pride. Daddy was right. Best to leave me here, out of sight.

He turned and started toward the house. Whining softly, Pride stood against the fence and watched him.

"Daddy?"

"What now?"

"Can Pride come in the house and sleep with me, just this one night? He wants to."

"That's a valuable animal, not a pet." But he hesitated and looked back at Pride and me. For once I didn't drop my head but returned his look and let my needs show. Usually I kept them hidden so no one could hurt me with them.

"Just this once," he said, and walked on into the house.

Pride had no collar, but I gripped a handful of his mane and together we ran across the yard and bounded into the house. Daddy settled himself in the living room and turned up the television, pushing Pride's head away, stroking it but pushing it away, too.

I dragged all of my boxes into the tiny square bedroom behind the living room. It was almost exciting to be settling permanently into this little room that was always mine on my summer visits. When the blue plastic radio was plugged in beside the bed and the horse and dog statues lined up on the windowsill, and all the clothes hung in the narrow closet

18

or laid in the dresser drawers, I turned the light off. The glow from the living room was enough to see by. I undressed and pulled my pajamas on and stretched out on the cot bed with its squeaky metal springs.

Remembered.

Got up and went into the cramped bathroom and took my yellow capsule. Pride followed me back into my room and stretched out beside me, taking most of the narrow bed. It felt wonderful.

From the living room I could hear the ten-o'clock news. It was a different channel from the one we listened to at home, Mom and me. Of course it would be different, this far south. They wouldn't get Chicago channels down here. St. Louis, this one sounded like. A strange voice, but I supposed I'd get used to it.

I fell asleep easily, as I always did, but by two o'clock I was wide awake. As I always was. A side effect of the medicine, the doctor had told me. Nothing to be done about it.

The house was absolutely still. No traffic noise from outside, like back home. The window near the foot of the bed was open, but even so there was no outdoor noise. Wait. Yes, the soft whirr of an owl. The rustle of some small creature across the grass, the tiger-striped cat maybe.

A tiny shard of a cry, like a splinter of glass, as cat or owl caught its field mouse and tore it to death.

I rolled over and wrapped both arms around Pride and buried my face in his mane. He stirred and crowded back against me. His length matched mine; his four white paws extended over the side of the cot. His tail thrashed once against the sheet and his front paws twitched.

Did he dream about being free? I wondered. Did he

19

spend his days and nights looking out through the fence that kept him safe, longing with all his soul to be free to race across the hay field and just keep going?

Inside me was a pool of love that I carried always, feeling the weight of it and needing to pour it out on someone or something who would want it, someone who would long to have it as much as I longed to give it. It couldn't be Mom because she was afraid of me, and she had had Mike. It couldn't be Daddy because he, too, was afraid of me, in some deeper way than Mom.

I stroked the hard silken side of the dog's face and felt the first trickling escape of my flood of love.

Three

Usually in the mornings I was thick-headed and sleepy from the hours of wakefulness during the night. But the next morning I buzzed with nerves.

"The bus comes by at ten to eight," Daddy said while we ate cold breakfasts. "I called the school last Friday and told them about you. They said they'd tell the bus driver to stop for you."

I picked up my dishes and put them in the sink. "Did you tell them about my . . ."

"No," he said gruffly, "but you're going to have to report in with the school nurse and let her know. She'll have to be prepared in case you have one of your . . . spells."

"I know it. I'll tell her."

I went outside to stand by the dirt road near Daddy's mailbox. My heart was pounding; I could feel it in my neck veins. An aura coming on? I stood very still and waited. The

21

terror was there, but not yet the overwhelming senseless terror of an aura. No . . . wait . . . no, it was all right. This was just a small passing terror, the same one I'd carried in the back of my mind for five years now, ever since my first grand mal seizure.

Before that the spells had been so small they were hardly noticeable even to me, a sudden brief spasm of twitching eyelid or chin, a few seconds of blankness like a small instant sleep in the middle of a conversation.

Then, one Saturday morning when I was eight, the grand mal happened. I'd been helping Mom empty wastebaskets into the trash bin behind our apartment building. As I lifted a wastebasket to tip it into the bin, I felt light-headed and uneasy, as though something terrible were about to happen. The sunlight grew unbearably bright. A ringing began in my ears and my head was filled with a dreadful stench, like rotting death.

The sunlight dimmed to a monochrome of grays and blacks around me, and I was smothered by a terror so overwhelming that it froze me in place, my arms still holding up the wastebasket.

I tried to call for Mom, but no sound came out.

As the black cloud engulfed me I disappeared from myself.

And then Mom's face was there, looking down at me, as terrified as I had just been. She and a neighbor helped me up from the ground and somehow got me up the steps and into the apartment, and later to the doctor's office. I was too sleepy to know or care where I was. The only thing that kept me awake was the nearly unbearable pain in my tongue where I had bitten it and on my forehead where I'd fallen against the trash bin. I didn't know that my mouth was flecked with foam and my pants soaked with urine. I only knew that I'd been through hell, literally had been through hell in my mind, and now I needed to sleep.

That was five years ago. In those five years it had happened six more times, usually in bed at night, but once just a few weeks ago on a Sunday afternoon when some of Mike's friends were over watching a ball game on television. I was on the floor in the living room, watching the game and enjoying the joking around, when I felt my aura starting, the brightness of the light and the first grip of the terror. I'd tried to get up, to get out of the room and away from the men, but they grabbed my wrist and teased me to bring them something from the kitchen. The seizure happened right there in front of all of Mike's buddies.

And within a week Mike had moved out. Oh, it was for other reasons, too, I knew that. He and Mom had been fighting over practically anything either one of them said. But I also knew how shaken Mike had been when I came to after that seizure, and I knew how he felt when his buddies decided to finish watching the game at somebody else's place. They all understood and felt sorry for me, but still they were uneasy around Mike after that, and especially around me.

And now the yellow school bus was coming at me down the road. It would trap me and carry me to a strange school where everyone knew everyone else, except me. I'd be stared at and talked about and wondered about until I was absorbed and familiar to them.

23

I was under orders to report to the school nurse and tell her I was epileptic, so she would know what was happening if I had a seizure at school. She would whisper it to the teachers so they could be prepared. They would look at me with caution and concern, and they would all wish they hadn't gotten stuck with me in their classes. No matter how kind and concerned they might be, they would still wish to be rid of me.

Because a seizure could happen anytime. At any moment in any class on any day, the lights could begin to brighten painfully, the rotten smell could fill my head, and the terror clouds could begin to gather and roll over me. I'd fall down, go stiff as a board, and then my arms and legs would start jerking and jumping. My eyes would roll and bubbles of foam would gather on my lips. Worst of all, I would wet my pants. I wouldn't know these things were happening, but everyone would see them. It would only last a minute or two, but that would be long enough to terrify every kid in the room, as well as the teacher, and maybe give them bad dreams for a long time afterward.

"Well, here we go," I told myself through gritted teeth. "Happy school days."

The bus rolled to a stop and I pulled myself up and into it.

Back home I'd lived two blocks from school, so this was my first time in a school bus. I didn't know what to expect, so I forced a smile onto my face and hoped for the best.

The driver was a big old guy. His head was bald, tanned and freckled from the sun. He looked as if he spent most of his time on a tractor, and probably he did.

He gave me a quick look and bellowed, "One, two, three."

From the busload of kids came a chorus of voices, "Hi, March Halsey. Welcome to Bus Fourteen. No yelling or hitting or spitting allowed."

"Hey, you done that real good," the driver called back to them.

I grinned at them all, a genuine grin this time, and sat down in the first empty seat I came to. It was next to a girl a little younger than me.

"He made us rehearse that speech a hundred times," the girl said.

"It was a great speech. Made me feel welcome." We smiled at each other, and everyone settled back into his or her own conversation.

This wasn't going to be bad, I decided.

Then I decided something else. I wasn't going to report in to the school nurse. I wasn't going to have all these new teachers talking about me over their lunches and getting scared for fear I was going to have a spell in their classes. With luck maybe a seizure wouldn't happen again for a long time, and then with some more luck it would be at night in my own room and maybe Daddy wouldn't even have to see it.

With luck.

It was the smallest school I'd ever seen, but it was pretty. It was built of blocks of cream-colored limestone, and the doors and window frames were painted dark green. The building looked at least a hundred years old. It was two stories tall, and down a half flight of stairs was a semi-basement where the gym and kitchen and offices were. There were only four rooms on each of the upstairs floors, with a broad central hall lined with lockers. Just the eight classrooms, and this was the whole junior and senior high school for Coalville, Illinois, and surrounding rural townships. I felt good about this school almost before I was inside it.

Just inside the front door stood an impressive-looking middle-aged woman, thin and beautifully dressed and groomed. She smiled when she saw me and held out her hand.

"March?"

"Yes."

"I'm Mrs. Snorff, the principal. Welcome to Coalville. Come into my office for just a minute while we get acquainted and work out your class schedule."

Her office was tiny and cramped and crowded with her secretary and a line of kids, but Mrs. Snorff settled me in a corner chair and picked up a new file folder. It had my name on it.

"Your records haven't arrived yet from your old school," she said, "so just tell me a little about yourself. March is such a striking name, so unusual. Is there a story behind it?"

I shrugged. "They were going to name me April but I was two weeks early getting born. I was due on April Fools' Day."

She smiled. "And you had just started seventh grade in Champaign, is that right?"

I nodded.

"All right. Well, I'm afraid this school is going to seem

26

very small in comparison, and we can't begin to offer the variety of classes a larger school could."

"That's not important," I said quickly. "It's so friendly here. On the bus this morning they all said a welcome speech when I got on. And at my old school I never even hardly saw the principal, let alone being greeted at the door."

She gave me a long, warm smile. "Good. I think you're going to fit right in, March. We can use your help on the junior-high girls' basketball team, for one thing. We barely have enough junior-high girls to make a team, and—"

"I don't do any sports stuff," I said quickly. I'd almost slipped and said "I can't" instead of "I don't."

"Oh. Well, we'll see how things go. Now, is there anything I should know about before we send you off to your first class?"

She met my eyes and I met hers. "No, I can't think of anything."

It was going to be on my school records. She was going to find out as soon as the records came in the mail. But at least I could have a few days to be a normal new girl before I had to start being March Halsey, the one with the seizures.

When I got home that afternoon I ran into the house intent on changing my clothes and getting out to the kennel as fast as I could. I barged into my bedroom and yelped, startled.

A woman stood there by the window, holding one of my horse statues.

She jumped, too, and put a hand to her throat. "My lord, girl, you like to scared me out of my hide."

It was Kathryn Gorsuch from across the road, and I could see now what she was doing. She had a dust cloth in one hand and a bandanna tied around her hair.

"Hi, Kathryn," I said shyly. She always affected me that way, and I wasn't sure why. It might have been because she was hard to catalog in my mind. Her father had been a doctor, and their house, across the road and up a little ways, was much bigger and nicer than our house. In fact, theirs had been the main farmhouse back when this whole area was one huge farm, and our house was for the hired man. So those things should have set Kathryn above Daddy and me, and yet she came over one day a week and cleaned house for Daddy and cooked up a bunch of food for the freezer, just like she was our hired help. That had never made sense to me.

Then, too, there was something strong about Kathryn that drew me to her, something quiet and strong in the center of her that I needed to have in me and didn't, and that made me shy of her, too. For a while, when I was younger, I'd had a crush on Kathryn, dreaming about her at night and daydreaming when I couldn't get to sleep. I imagined her hugging me and holding me and saying wonderful loving things to me. She never did or said any of those things, and yet I felt nurtured by her anyway, just being near her.

I gave her a hug and she patted my back with the dust cloth.

"I see you got some new ones," she said, holding up the bronze horse. "How did it go at school your first day? They treat you okay?"

"Yeah, great. On the bus this morning they all recited

this welcome speech. It went, 'Welcome to Bus Fourteen. No yelling or hitting or spitting allowed.'"

Kathryn laughed with me, a big, deep belly laugh with no holds barred.

"And then the principal met me at the door and welcomed me personally. They'd sure never do that back in my old school. And the teachers were all real nice. The classes were so small, I couldn't get over it. Only twelve kids in the whole seventh grade. Only about eighty in the whole junior and senior high together. I knew everybody's name in my whole class by lunchtime."

Kathryn went on with her dusting, doing the whole tiny room in what looked like a continuous sweep. Two minutes with the vacuum cleaner and my room was done. I followed her into the kitchen and sat on the counter while she took a casserole from the oven, divided it into small plastic dishes, and stored them in the freezer on the laundry porch.

"I'm glad to hear you talk that way," Kathryn said. She stood at the sink and began washing and peeling potatoes. "I was kind of worried about you, your first day in a new school and all."

"Why would you worry?" I stared apprehensively at her. She didn't know about my epilepsy; at least I didn't think so. I'd never had a seizure here at the farm, and Daddy would never tell anybody about it if he didn't have to.

"Oh, you just kind of like to keep to yourself, times you've been here for vacations. You never seemed like much of a one for playing with neighbor children, and like-a-that. Always seemed to want to be by yourself or off with the dogs. I didn't know how you'd get on, first day in a new school, that's all. I'm glad it went okay for you." She sliced off a piece of potato and levered it into my mouth from the knife. It was woody and wet and crisp.

"You used to eat off my paring knife like a little bird when you were younger," she said. "Little sparrow, you were."

"How come you never had any children of your own, Kathryn? Didn't you want any?"

She gave me a long, cool look, as if I'd trespassed on private territory. Then she went on peeling and slicing. "Never got married, that's why."

"Why didn't you?"

"None of your business."

"Did you have a boyfriend?"

"Oh yeah, I had one or two in my day. None I wanted to keep, though."

"None? Not any?"

She sniffed and didn't answer.

"You'd better get your clothes changed and get outside, let your daddy know you're home. I expect he'll be wanting to know how your first day went."

I braced my arms to swing down off the counter. Then I took a slow look at Kathryn. She had a big square face almost like mine, and sandy hair. A heavy chin and a thick, mannish nose. She was the one who should have been my mother.

"I'm glad you didn't have any kids of your own," I said suddenly. I hadn't meant to say it out loud. I was just thinking how jealous I'd have been if she had her own children to love and take care of.

"What a thing to say." She gave me a scoffing look and a small shove that swung me off the counter.

I found Daddy inside the kennel, grooming one of the dogs. It was the first time I'd seen the inside of the building, and I loved it. With double doors standing open at either end of the long central alleyway, it reminded me of pictures of stables I'd seen in horse magazines. The kennel had the same rows of stalls along either side, with beautiful animals looking out at me over the doors. Only everything here was scaled down for dogs instead of horses; there were runs instead of paddocks. Halfway down the alleyway, where a stable would have had its tack room, there was an open space cluttered with wire show crates and grooming tables. A fluorescent overhead light brightened the area. Set high on the rough plank wall, on a brace just under the eaves, was a small brown radio playing country-western music.

Daddy didn't turn down the music as I came to stand near the table where I could watch. He looked at me, then concentrated on the dog that stood on the low grooming table.

"Which one is this, again?" I asked. He'd named all the dogs for me last night, but there had been so many.

Daddy sniffed. "Baron. The pick of Pride's first litter. Got him entered at Danville this weekend. How'd it go today? Have any problems at school?"

"No, it was fine. Everybody was real nice to me. Can I help?"

He went on stroking the dog's side with a slicker brush as though he hadn't heard, but finally he reached across Baron's back and handed the brush to me.

31

"Don't go in too deep," he said. "Don't want to pull out any more undercoat than we have to. Just go over his britches and leg furnishings for mats."

The dog was a very dark mahogany sable, a rich red tipped with black. He looked like old polished wood. His neck carried the same broad, white shawl collar as Pride's, and he had white strips running up the front edges of his hind legs.

"I like this white on his back legs," I said as I stroked upward through the profuse "britches" of hair beneath his tail.

"That means he's white factored," Daddy said. "Any collie that's got white all the way up his stifles like that carries the gene to produce white pups."

"White?"

Daddy moved to the dog's head and began dabbing gray claylike stuff onto Baron's inner ears, just a tiny touch to make the ears fall forward perfectly. He didn't answer me, but I could see his face relaxing.

With Daddy, dogs were the key. I'd sensed it before, but I knew it for sure as he began to talk to me about white collies and how to breed them. He wasn't especially thinking about me. I was just somebody he could talk to about dogs, somebody as eager to learn as he was to teach. As long as I let him teach me about dogs, and as long as we both ignored what was wrong with me, we'd get along fine. And since I truly wanted to learn about the dogs, that part would be easy.

In my mind I slammed the door on the knowledge that sooner or later he was going to see me having a seizure and

32

then it might be all over. He'd think up some excuse and send me back to Mom, who didn't want me either.

I thought about the new school, so small and friendly and glad to have me. I thought about the kennel, the dogs, Pride, whom I could love because he loved and accepted me. I thought about having Kathryn just across the road every day of my life for the next three years.

It would kill me to leave here, I realized, surprised. Only one day and already I knew I wanted to stay here forever.

It all depended on Daddy. Was he the kind of person who could still feel the same about me after he'd seen a seizure? I didn't know. He was a stranger to me, a tall, narrow-faced stranger in overalls and a plaid shirt. He held such power over me, over my life and happiness, and I hardly knew him at all.

He was saying, ". . . mahogany sables like this one, that means they carry the recessive color gene for tricolor. The light golden sables like Honey, they're pure for sable, and if you want to get darker color you have to cross with a tri or a mahogany, see?"

He paused, his small scissors poised over the edge of one collie ear; his eyes caught mine and looked into them, startlingly deep.

"I see. So if you breed two mahogany sables together, what would you get?"

His scissors returned to their snipping. "Could get mahoganies, goldens, tricolors, and if both of them was white-factored on top of it you could get sable-headed whites, tri-headed whites . . ."

A feeling of overwhelming contentment came over me. For the moment I felt . . . safe.

Four

"You go on over to Kathryn's if you get lonesome or scared now, hear?"

"I will, but I won't," I said.

Daddy looked up at me through the window of his station wagon. He was wearing clothes I'd never seen before, wool slacks and a nice shirt and a leather cap, one of those squashed-forward ones like a rich Englishman would wear. He didn't even look like my dad.

In the back of the car was a wire dog crate with Baron lying inside, a folding table to groom him on, and two overnight bags, one for Daddy and one full of dog stuff. They were off for Danville, where Baron was entered the next day in his first show.

I'd been waiting and hoping all week for Daddy to mention my going with him. I didn't ask to be included; the important thing was for him to want me without my having to ask. But all he asked was whether I'd be afraid to stay alone for two days and a night. I said I wouldn't be. He relaxed and began showing me the kennel routine so Kathryn wouldn't have to do it, as she usually did when he went on dog show trips.

Once I'd gotten over the disappointment at being left out, I began looking forward to these two days of solitude. By the time Daddy rolled his car window up and drove out the lane and down the road, I was elated.

It was early Saturday afternoon, and I was gloriously free. I'd spent the morning cramming away at my homework, and by now the chapters were all read and the five-hundred-word theme completed. What a dancing feeling that was!

The air was hot and heavy and fragrant from the field across the road, where a neighbor was cutting clover hay. Just beyond the corner of the hay field Kathryn's lawn began. I could see her in baggy shorts and a man's shirt, pushing her lawn mower along the shallow roadside ditch.

I'd never been at the farm in late September before, and I was delighted to find that summer stretched this late into the year. Up in Champaign the trees would already be starting to turn colors.

I stood in the farm lane for minutes, immobilized by my choices. For the first time in my life there was no one watching me or directing my activity. It was intoxicating. I could go back into the house and read one of the library books I'd brought home yesterday. I could try cooking something, like a cake or brownies. I could go to the kennel and get out any dog I wanted and brush it. I could go exploring somewhere.

While I debated, a figure on a bicycle appeared around

the curve of the road beyond Kathryn's house. It waved at me. I waved back, squinting to see who it was. It was one of the girls in my class, the one who rode Bus Fourteen with me. Karen. We'd ridden together Thursday afternoon coming home, and again yesterday. She'd been openly friendly in an intelligent way, and I'd felt the first glow of friendship aborning.

She coasted to a stop beside the mailbox. She was tall and heavy-boned, with dark, curly hair and huge, blue eyes. Her voice was soft, with just the trace of a childhood lisp that she worked hard to hide.

"I was trying to call you," she said. "You must not have heard the phone."

"I was outside. Where are you going?"

"Swimming. That's why I was calling you. Come with me, can you? It's not really swimming, just a place where the river bends that's deep enough to splash around in. Get your suit and come on. Do you have a bike?"

"No," I said sadly, not for the lack of a bike but for the tantalizing idea of swimming in the river with Karen. With anybody, anywhere, just swimming. "I can't go. I wish I could."

"Won't your dad let you?"

"No. Well, he's gone for the weekend. That's not it."

"What, then? Come on, you can go just for a little while, can't you? If you have chores I'll help you with them after we swim. Come on, it's no fun going alone, and my brothers are cutting hay today. Come on, go with me."

"I really can't. I'm sorry."

Karen studied my face for a long, still moment, weighing

me. She'd made a difficult move, an open gesture of friendship to a new person, and that person was turning her down for no apparent reason. I could almost read her thoughts in her wide-open face: disappointment, embarrassment, hurt feelings because I'd rejected her offer, her friendship.

"I wish I could," I said fervently.

"Then why can't you?" Her eyes met mine and held them in a sad kind of challenge. Instinctively I knew that this was a crucial moment. If Karen rode away hurt and angry I might never have a close friend here. If I risked the truth . . . the same danger. She might use it against me.

Karen's face cooled and hardened. She prepared to push off.

"There is a reason," I said quickly. "I'm not supposed to swim because of my condition and swimming could be dangerous. I didn't want people to know about it." My voice trailed off to a near-whisper.

"What condition?" She looked doubtful of my honesty.

Oh boy, here goes nothing. Here goes everything. I closed my eyes and forced the words out.

"I have epilepsy. I take medication that's supposed to keep the . . . seizures . . . under control, but it doesn't always work, and if I had a seizure while I was in the water I'd drown. My mother doesn't even like me to take tub baths, but I cheat sometimes. Nobody around here knows about this except my dad, and I'd really . . ."

I ran out of breath and courage, so I just leaned into her gaze and trusted her. It was the hardest thing I'd ever done in my life.

She looked at me for a full minute without saying anything or changing her expression. When she finally opened her mouth I felt dizzy with fear.

"I used to have a terrible speech impediment," she said. Her tone was carefully casual, as though she understood my fragility.

I nodded, not trusting my voice.

Suddenly Karen took a long breath and said, "Listen, get on the back and I'll ride you down to the river. You can wade in the shallow part if you want to, or sit on the bank and keep me company, or go in the deep part and I'll watch out for you. I'm bigger than you are. I won't let you drown."

That afternoon I was conscious of a happiness so intense that I knew I would remember the day always. With my hands locked on Karen's waist and my legs wide-straddled, we bounced down the road laughing at nothing. We left the bike in the ditch beside a small bridge and slid down the weedy bank to the water's edge. There we pulled our shoes off and waded upstream to a place where the river curved and deepened in a band of willows and cottonwood trees. The river bottom was sandy, the water barely up to my knees.

Karen showed me her river, safely shallow on this side of the little sandbar, deeper and faster on the far side of it, but nowhere was it more than waist deep. She plunged on into the darker green water; I waded and crouched in the safer side.

When we were soaked and refreshed and winded, we sat on the sandbar and talked.

"What does it feel like," she asked shyly, "when you have a . . . you know. . . ."

"A seizure." I trusted her now, so I spoke matter-of-factly. "Well, in the first place they don't happen very often, maybe once a year, and the rest of the time I'm just like anyone else. Except I can't sleep more than a few hours at night because the medication keeps me awake, so lots of times I get sleepy in the afternoons. I have an awful time staying awake in school sometimes."

She grinned. "Me, too, and I don't have a good excuse like you do. But I mean, what does it feel like . . ."

"I don't feel it at all when it's actually happening. I'm unconscious. It only lasts a minute or two. The bad parts are before and after. I get an aura just before it happens. It's called an aura, I don't know why. I get this terrible feeling that I can't explain. It's like I'm terrified out of my mind, but not for any reason. And everything gets very bright and then sort of dim and gray, and I smell some horrible smell like, I don't know, rotting or something. If I have time I try to lie down wherever I am, just so I don't fall and hurt myself. Then I go blank, and when I come to I'm so sleepy I can't stay awake, usually for about a day afterward, and my muscles are so sore I can hardly get out of bed. That's because while I'm in the seizure my muscles go rigid, really hard, and then they jerk around and I guess it's hard on the muscles or something."

Karen was silent for a long time, gazing into the screen of willows across the river. "Wow," she whispered finally. "That must be awful, not ever knowing when it might happen."

"Mmm."

Minutes slid past with the twinkling flow of river water. We mesmerized ourselves staring into it.

39

"Teach me how to swim, will you?" I said after a while. I took off my shirt and shorts and waded into the deep water with my hand on Karen's shoulder.

The evening was almost as good as the afternoon. When I got back from swimming—swimming!—I fed and watered all of the dogs, then brought Pride into the house for company. I opened a can of spaghetti and ate the whole canful sitting in the living room and reading while I ate. This seemed a marvelous luxury, to be able to disappear into a story while I ate, rather than talking or being silent with another person. There was a level of tension about eating with someone else that I had never recognized until now, by its absence.

Feeling gleefully wicked, I let Pride lick the sauce off my plate when I was finished. He kissed me with tomato breath and I loved him.

After supper I did the dishes and straightened and dusted the whole house just to use up energy. Then, just for fun, I took the blankets off my bed and made a nest for Pride and me on the davenport in the living room. With the lights off and the television on, we curled up and watched and dozed. When my two o'clock wakefulness hit, there was a late-night movie going on right in front of me. Another wonderful new luxury. Before the movie was finished I was asleep again and stayed that way till morning.

I made waffles for breakfast, one for me and one for Pride. Then I spent the rest of the morning in the kennel with the radio playing fast music. I cleaned all of the runs and checked the water buckets, then turned one batch of dogs at a time out for a run in the big fenced yard behind the kennel. They raced around the yard like kids, snatching sticks from each other's mouths, crashing into one another for the fun of it.

While they took turns in the yard, I brushed Pride and several of the others, pretending I was grooming them for a dog show. They loved the attention.

After lunch Kathryn came over and helped me get the lawn mower started. She stayed the whole time I was mowing, for company or for safety. She sat in a folding chair on the shady side of the lawn while I went back and forth, back and forth, back and forth. I did the house yard all the way out to the road, and with leftover energy I did all the little grassy areas around and between the buildings. Then I picked up three million dog-chunks from the exercise yard and mowed in there. Daddy hadn't mowed it all summer, judging from the tangle of weedy grass. When I was finished it was beautiful.

Three o'clock. At the dog show, collies were scheduled to be judged at one in the afternoon. Daddy had said he'd be through by two and home by six or seven. As eager as I was to find out how Baron did, I hated to see the last few hours of freedom drift away.

Swimming would be wonderful. The afternoon had become sticky hot, with thunderclouds starting to gather in the west. But Karen had said she'd be helping with the haying today, and to go swimming alone was just plain dangerous for me.

Sighing, I washed the sweat and mowing dust off my face and arms and settled in the lawn chair with my book.

Five o'clock. Reluctantly I laid the book facedown and stood and stretched and went toward the kennel. I'd give the runs one more cleaning just so they'd be extra good when Daddy got home, then feed the dogs and get myself some supper.

When I came around the corner by Pride's run, I knew something was wrong. All of the dogs were standing quietly, staring at something in one of the far runs. It was a dog, lying very still.

I ran.

It was a big, gangly, golden sable male, a litter brother to Baron. He lay on his side, his belly swollen. I didn't have to touch him to know he was dead.

No. Oh no, please.

I felt his face: cold and stiffening. His mouth was open, his eyes drying.

My stomach lurched, then held. I ran into the house and dialed the phone number at the top of the emergency list taped to the wall.

"Hardy," a gruff masculine voice answered.

"Dr. Hardy?"

"Yes?"

"This is Clinton Halsey's daughter. One of our collies is dead. I don't know what happened. I just went out there to clean the runs and he was lying there dead. What should I do?"

"You sure he's dead? What'd he look like?"

I told him.

"Well," the man said, "nothing much I can do about it. If you want him posted, bring him in in the morning."

I hung up, frantic with unanswered needs. Kathryn. Ignoring the greater convenience of the telephone, I bolted out of the house and ran up the road to pound on her back door.

"One of the dogs died," I panted.

She brought me in and sat me down. "What happened? Take a deep breath. No, don't try to talk till you get your breath. Are you sure it's dead?"

"Maybe not. He looked dead, but maybe not. Come and look at him."

Together we walked back down the road at her speed, slower than my frantic pace. She stood over the dog and looked down at him with her implacable face.

"You're right, he's dead. No doubt about that."

"But what from? Poison? What? Was it my fault?"

She stooped suddenly and lifted the long, limp dog in her arms and carried him out of the run. "You go call the vet and tell him we're bringing a dog in to be posted, and I'll go get my car."

"I already called him," I wailed. "He told me if I wanted—what did you call it? Posted?—if I wanted him posted, to bring him in the morning. It's Sunday night. He won't want to . . ."

She glared at me. "A posting ought to be done as soon as possible if he's going to find out what the dog died of. You go back in there and call him back and tell him we're on our way. I'll be right back with the car. No, come to think of it, you'd better stay home in case your daddy gets back early. I'll take the dog in and come back here. I'm sure it wasn't anything that was your fault, honey, but I'll be here as soon as I can, just in case he's looking for someone to take it out on."

After she'd driven off I remembered the other dogs. I fed them fast and refilled water buckets, then went into Pride's stall inside the kennel and sat with him. The stalls had swinging doors so the dogs could go out into their runs whenever they wanted to, but he stayed with me.

Six o'clock. Daddy could be home anytime. Kathryn should be back from town any minute now. I knew I should get up, but it was so comfortable there in Pride's straw bedding, with his warm woolly mass beside me.

Suddenly he stood up and put his face close to mine, sniffing and whining softly. He pawed lightly at my chest as though trying to tell me something.

And then I knew. The kennel grew dazzlingly bright, and the terror and stench came toward me, came into my head. I reached for Pride.

Gentle moisture was stroking my face; I struggled to focus my eyes. Pride's face was against mine, his tongue cleaning the spittle from my chin. I could feel the warmth of his body along my own, and the comfort of it eased me back to full consciousness more smoothly and surely than ever before.

"March, are you all right, honey?"

A woman's voice. I was too disoriented, too sleepy to recognize her. I moved my arm and saw that my fist held a thatch of black collie hair. Still Pride pressed himself against me.

"I'm okay," I tried to say, but my jaw was numb and my

44

tongue thick and full of pain. I'd bitten it again. I dreaded the next week or so while the untreatable pain diminished.

Kathryn's arms supported me from behind and moved me by slow steps toward the house. As always after a seizure, I had the sensation of having been far away for a very long time. I barely recognized the house before my eyes.

Kathryn was talking, but I couldn't concentrate long enough to follow her.

"Pride," I said loud and clear around my swollen tongue.

We hesitated. Kathryn set me down on the ground and left me for a moment. Sleep . . . I sagged to the left. She was back again, picking me up, moving me forward, but this time my dog was at my other side.

"Sorry," I said with a lopsided smile as I held up the swatch of hair still clenched in my fist.

Bed. It was my only aim. The pillowcase was against my nose. Kathryn was doing something to me, pulling my clothes off and arranging my arms and legs under the sheet. Dimly I felt her pry open my mouth to look at my tongue, felt her dab something on it. That was okay. I didn't care, just so the bed stayed under me and Pride stayed where he was, stretched out against me. I could think tomorrow. Not now.

Not now. . . .

Five

It was late afternoon before I was fully awake. Hours earlier I'd heard a distant voice say, "Let her sleep. Call the school and say she has the flu. She needs to rest."

My exhaustion was real enough. Although the seizures lasted only a few minutes, the mental activity and muscular tension were so superhuman during those minutes that there was simply nothing left to go on with. I welcomed the escape of sleep. I'd bitten my tongue before, and I knew the pain that lay in wait for me. Even a few days from now, when the worst was over, it would stab me again with every attempt to eat or talk.

And worse than that, there was Daddy to face. The dead dog.

Every time I began to waken I forced myself back down into sleep. But finally my eyes opened of their own will and stayed open in spite of my wishes.

Kathryn was there. She was sitting in a living-room chair just beyond my bedroom door, reading. When I stirred she got up and came to stand beside the bed.

"How are you feeling, honey?"

I pointed to my mouth and shook my head slightly.

"I know. Don't try to talk. What do you need? Bathroom?"

I nodded. She steadied me into the bathroom and waited to walk me back to the bed. Actually, I didn't feel badly now that I was up and moving, except for my mouth. I got dressed and went to sit at the kitchen table while Kathryn started some pork chops sizzling.

"Will you be able to eat supper?" she asked me.

"Drink it," I said. The pain was ferocious.

"Soup then, for you. How come you never told me you were epileptic?"

I shrugged and looked away from her sharp gaze.

"Oh well, I reckon it's not a subject you bring up if you don't have to. Ted was like that, too. It nearly killed him to have to admit he was less than perfect. Well, I reckon it did kill him, in the end, didn't it?"

I looked puzzled.

"Your uncle Ted," she said impatiently.

Uncle Ted? I didn't know I had one. My expression must have shown my thoughts.

"You knew about your uncle Ted, didn't you? Your father's brother?"

I shook my head blankly.

Kathryn's expression grew guarded. "Oh well, then, I'd best not be gossiping. You can ask your dad about him."

But I needed to know, now. I forced my tongue to form, "Ted? Epi. . . ?"

"Yeah. He had it, too."

"Daddy . . . saw him?"

She had to think about that before she understood. "Saw him have seizures, you mean? Oh yes. Several times. We both did. The three of us were very close, growing up, Teddy and Clint and I. Teddy was . . . very special. A very special person."

Her face softened for just an instant, but it was long enough to tell me something she would never have told me with words. Kathryn had loved my uncle Ted when they were young together. Maybe she still did. Maybe that was why she never got married and had children of her own.

"What . . . happened?"

"Died. Your dad can tell you about it if he wants you to know. Now then, what's your pleasure, tomato? Cream of chicken? Chicken noodle?" She stood before the cupboard and read labels to me.

"Cream."

"Of chicken, right?"

I nodded.

"Dog," I said.

"Oh yes. Almost forgot about that. Well, we don't know yet what the doc found out. Your dad had to go work at the sale barn today, said he'd check at the vet's on his way home. Ought to be here pretty quick now. Listen, I've got to be getting on home. You're feeling okay now?"

I nodded.

"Good, then. Just watch that those chops don't cook dry.

48

Add a little water, give them about a half hour, and by that time the potatoes'll be baked. You can heat up a can of beans or something. Here now, your soup's done, just warm, not too hot for your poor tongue."

She set the bowl of soup down, looked at me, and pulled me in for a long hug. Her sympathy almost undid my grip on my own self-pity. Then she gave me a brisk pat, almost a spank, and left without another word, letting the screen door slam behind her.

Daddy had just driven in. I could hear their voices out in the yard but couldn't make out the words.

I braced against his probable bad mood. From past experience I knew that Mondays and Thursdays, when he worked at the local livestock sale barn—hog sales every Monday, cattle every Thursday—he was always depressed. I didn't know whether it was because he didn't like the work itself or didn't want to work for someone else and admit he wasn't making enough money here on the farm.

Already I was beginning to understand my father a little bit. I understood that he was a bigger man inside his head an he was on the outside. I could hear it when he bragged about his dogs, could hear the statement he was making: Clinton Halsey is a man of substance and importance. Breeder of champion show dogs. Owner of Halsey's Kennels. I could see it in that fancy leather cap he wore driving off to the show.

So naturally he'd hate having to go off every Monday and Thursday and spend hours being a pig driver and calf herder at the sale barn. He wanted Clinton Halsey to be better than that.

On top of that, he had a dead dog and a kid with fits to think about.

Quickly I got up from my soup and set his place at the table. I stabbed the baking potatoes, opened a can of peas, poured a shot of water in the skillet to keep the chops alive.

When he came in I was looking as normal and healthy as I possibly could. He gave me a nod, an expressionless look, and went on through to the bathroom, leaving a trail of pig smell in the air.

He came back, damp and smelling better. "How long till supper? I ought to feed them dogs. I don't reckon you did them, did you?"

I shook my head. "Fifteen minutes." My words sounded thick, like I was drunk.

He looked at me oddly for a second. "Oh yeah, you've got a sore tongue, don't you? You feeling okay otherwise?"

I nodded and smiled.

"Good, then. I'll go do the dogs."

While he was gone a cheering thought came to me. If Daddy had grown up with an epileptic brother, then I could quit worrying about him not being able to take it if I had a seizure in front of him. I'd started to grasp that thought earlier, when Kathryn was talking, but had lost it in the recognition of the love in her voice when she mentioned Ted.

Daddy came in again and we ate without talking. This was another thing I'd learned about him. He could eat or talk, but not both at once, and when he settled into a meal he didn't want to be bothered with conversation.

So I waited apprehensively until his pork chops were slivers of bone and his potatoes just discarded skins.

"The dog?" I asked finally.

"Torsion."

"What?"

He looked at me across the table then and explained. "He died of stomach torsion. I had another one die of it just a couple months ago, so Doc knew where to look this time, and sure enough, that's what it was. It wasn't nothing that could have been prevented. Just an accident."

Relief washed over me.

He went on in his teaching voice. "What it is, is like, say this dish towel is a dog's stomach." He took a towel from the sink, stretched it between his hands, then with a quick circular motion swung it like a jump rope, just once. The towel hung twisted between his hands.

"That's what torsion is. Sometimes a dog's stomach can flip clear over, just like that dish towel. Maybe he just ate a heavy meal or took a big drink of water, so there's weight in his stomach, see. Then maybe he gets to jumping around, barking at something or whatever. That stomach swings around in there, and all of a sudden it flips clean over. What that does is it seals off the top and bottom openings into that stomach. Gases build up in there just like in a balloon, and in about twenty, thirty minutes the pressure is so great the stomach explodes and the dog dies."

I stared, sickened.

He tossed the towel to the counter and shrugged. "Well, if you're going to breed stock of any kind, you're going to lose a few now and then. I'm sorry it happened when you were here alone, but it didn't have anything to do with you."

51

I nodded and waited for him to mention my seizure. He didn't.

Finally I said, "Baron? Show?"

Daddy's face lit up then. He leaned back in his chair and crossed his legs and lit a cigarette. "We did good. He won his puppy class and got Reserve in the Winners class. Second out of fourteen. Darn good for a ten-month-old pup his first time out. He showed like a trooper, too. Moved out fast and straight, tail wagging the whole time. Nothing scared him, not the crowds nor the judge going over him, nor anything. He's going to be a natural showman, just like old Pride. God, it was a thrill going into the ring with that old Pride dog."

He smoked and daydreamed while I washed the dishes. As I was wiping off the table and countertops, he said, "You know what I was thinking, March? I was thinking, with you to help me, we could take a whole load of dogs up to the specialty in January."

"Specialty?"

"The Illiana Collie Fanciers' big annual specialty show. All collies, couple of hundred of them. We could take Baron, of course, maybe a couple of the younger pups for the Puppy Sweepstakes, and we'll take old Pride. Show him in the Stud Dog class and the Specials class. That's for champions. Would you like that? You could help me show them. I'll teach you how."

I glowed and grinned and nodded. It didn't occur to me until much later that this might have been a gift from him.

About a month later I had another seizure, but it happened on a Friday night, so no one but Daddy knew about it.

Pride was in the house with me at the time, and again he came to me whining just before the aura began. Remembering the last time, I pulled off one of my socks and stuffed it in my mouth as I lay down on the bed. The seizure was brief and light, and thanks to the sock I didn't bite my tongue this time. Again, Pride lay close against me until I was conscious again, and cleaned my face with his tongue. I found immense comfort in his presence, much more than in any human presence. The dog accepted and loved me without question or revulsion.

A few days later Karen and I were eating lunch side by side in the school gym, which doubled as a lunchroom. We were in the last shift, and already the far tables were being cleared and folded away. A few of the kids were shooting baskets, boys against girls.

Across the table from us, Angie Peltzer turned her back to us to watch the game. She was the tallest girl in our class and played forward on the girls' junior-high basketball team. They had started practice last week.

Angie said, "March, you ought to go out for basketball. Why don't you?"

"Too short," I said.

"Nah, you're not. You'd make a decent guard, anyhow. Lots of kids on the junior-high teams aren't very tall. Why don't you? Come on."

"I'm pretty busy after school with dog chores," I said, hoping that would be enough.

"Practice is only an hour after school, and you could ride home with Karen. Her mom always picks her up, and they live right up the road from you. You'd have time. Don't spend so much time doing homework."

She grinned at me. Angie and I were running about neck and neck for top grades in our class, and I knew she'd love to beat me. She didn't know that I often used my sleepless night hours to read ahead of assignments or to write papers that I knew would be assigned later on. I did it as part of my fight to hold my ground, because often I was so drugged with sleep in the afternoons that I couldn't concentrate on what the teachers were saying.

I guessed that Mrs. Snorff had received my school records long before now and that they included my having epilepsy, but I didn't know whether that word had been passed on to any of my teachers. I couldn't see that they treated me differently from the others, but with teachers it was hard to tell sometimes.

There was another reason I pushed so hard to get top grades. I needed to have that to fall back on. Once the word got out about me, it was crucial that the other kids already have a solid base of liking and respect for me. Then there was the chance that they might be able to absorb the bad part of me along with the good. Otherwise I would be written off. Shunted aside. I'd be one of the ones it's best to avoid.

Angie was looking at me. "Why don't you, March? At least try out for the team. You might not be good enough to make it, but if you're too chicken to even try out . . ."

Suddenly Karen flared. "Leave her alone, Angela." She said the name hard and hatefully. "If March doesn't want to play basketball she doesn't have to. Being good at one sport is plenty for anybody, and I happen to know March Halsey can swim circles around anyone in this school, including me. So just shut up and leave her alone, all right?"

Angie lifted her eyebrows and wrinkled her nose in a "get a load of you" expression. Haughtily she rose, emptied her tray in the trash barrel, and went to join the ball game at the other end of the room.

Karen and I looked at each other for a long, silent moment. Then I exploded in laughter with her.

"Swim circles around you?" I gasped.

"Well, you did. That day we went swimming in the river. Remember? You swam in a circle around me. Would I lie?"

Through helpless laughter I said, "I swam circles around you because you were holding me up, nut. I'd have sunk like a rock if you hadn't been holding me up."

"Oh well, Angie doesn't need to know that."

That afternoon I asked the bus driver to drop me in front of Kathryn's house instead of my own. I was in one of my moods and wasn't good company for myself.

She was in her living room, reading the same book she'd been reading that day after my seizure. It was a huge volume, a history of World War II.

"Why are you reading that?" I asked as I settled on the davenport and pulled an afghan around myself. The day was cold and dark; I needed to wrap myself in something warm and bright, even though the house was comfortable.

"War fascinates me," she said, laying the book facedown across her lap. "I keep studying all the wars in history, trying to figure out what it is that really starts them. Why do we keep doing this stupid, destructive thing century after century? If the people running the world know how wars have always been in the past, I can't imagine why they ever start new ones. How was your day?"

I sighed. "Okay, I guess. But they're after me to join the basketball team because it's such a little school they need all the players they can get. And I can't tell them why I can't play."

"Why can't you?"

I stared at her. "You know."

"Oh, that. Well, you're okay most of the time. What are the chances of your having a seizure during a game? Not so big, are they? If it's something you want to do, you ought to do it and not whine about it."

She was in a mood herself, I realized. Maybe this was just a bad day for everybody.

"It's not just the games," I said defensively. "It's an hour's practice every afternoon after school, and shower time and talks from the coach and all that. And I'm having more seizures now than I used to. They're coming about once a month, and that's way more than it used to be. And I'm taking my medicine every day, but it's just not working like it used to."

"That's a shame," she said, but her voice was distant, her thoughts somewhere else. Suddenly I needed her sympathy intensely. I needed her to come over on the davenport and hug me and tell me how brave I was.

"Why did this have to happen to me?" I asked. "What did I do to deserve this rotten condition anyhow? Why? Why me?"

She gave me a long level look. "Why not you?"

Her voice was quiet and even, but the words dropped like rocks on my heart. I stared at her, open-mouthed.

"Think about it," she said. "Just think about that for a while, girl."

56

Stiff with hurt, I unwound the afghan from my legs and rose. "I have to go home and take care of the dogs."

"Come again," she called, as she always did. I looked back from the door and saw that she had already picked up her book again.

I hated her.

Six

Early in December my supply of Dilantin ran low. The drugstore wouldn't renew the prescription without a doctor's okay, and the local doctor wouldn't give it to me over the phone. If I hadn't had a checkup in six months, he scolded, then I was overdue. Grumbling under my breath, I made the appointment.

I knew kids who had never gone to doctors in their whole lives, except to get the shots you need when you start school. Bitterly I envied them as I walked up the steps and into Dr. Graves's office.

Why me? I thought again, furious at whoever was responsible for creating me this way.

"Why not you?" Kathryn's voice echoed through my head. I refused to look at the inherent logic beneath her words.

It was an old-fashioned doctor's office in a wing built onto a large old house just off Coalville's main street. But the doctor was better than I'd hoped for. He was young middle-aged, small and skinny and dark.

He did all the usual tests, disappeared for half an hour, then called me back into the office part of the place and sat me down for a talk.

My tests were all more or less normal, he said, nothing to be concerned about. He explained several things I'd been wondering about. "Some people feel very tired after a seizure and need to sleep a lot. Some people experience muscle soreness, too, while others don't." Was I having any problems, anything unusual in my pattern of seizures?

"They're coming a lot more often than they used to," I said. "About once a month instead of once every six months. Why doesn't the Dilantin stop them? What's the point of taking it?"

He looked down at my record sheet and nodded to himself. "You're thirteen, right? Have you begun menstruating?"

I flushed. Even though I knew he was a doctor, that was a hard subject to talk about with a man. "Yes, just a couple of months ago. Why? Would that have something to do with the seizures?"

"Yes, actually it does, although we don't understand just why. The menstrual cycle does seem to trigger seizures in some people, so if I were you I'd be prepared for that to happen."

"Prepared!" I said angrily. "How can you be prepared if you never know when it's going to happen? Are you telling me I'm going to be having these damned things every

59

month for the rest of my life, no matter what medicine I take?" I couldn't stand the thought.

He smiled sympathetically. Sure, that was easy for him. He didn't have to go through this. "Probably not that long, but I'd say at least for the next few years and maybe throughout your menstruating years. We'll try increasing your dosage and see if that helps."

I stared at him hopelessly. Thirty, forty years of this ahead of me. "Is there any chance I'll outgrow it, Dr. Graves? My old doctor back home kept telling Mom it was just a childhood epilepsy and I'd outgrow it, but he was the kind of doctor who'd look a corpse in the eye and tell him he was getting better."

Dr. Graves threw back his head and laughed. Then, sobering, he said, "Some epileptic children do outgrow it, some don't, and there's absolutely no way of knowing ahead of time. All we can do is try to keep the seizures under control, keep you out of dangerous situations."

"Like swimming?"

"Swimming, driving a car, that sort of thing, yes. Drinking, when you get older, that'll be out. Smoking could be dangerous. Oh well, we have plenty of time to talk about those things. You're only thirteen."

I felt at least a hundred as I stood up to leave.

"Oh, one other thing I wanted to ask you about," I said at the door. "The last couple of seizures, my dog was with me when it happened, and it seemed like he could tell even before I could. He sort of whined and acted worried, and then I'd start getting my aura. Was that my imagination or can dogs really tell?"

"It's quite possible. I've heard of that sort of thing before,

60

a pet dog or cat giving warning. With their highly developed senses of smell and hearing and their sensitivity to changes in air pressure before a storm, I think it's entirely plausible that an animal might be picking up on some change in you, maybe an altered body scent. Some people say we all have a colored aura around our body all the time that human eyes can't register but animal eyes can, and that our aura changes color when our moods change. It could be such a change that pets react to. At any rate, if I were you I'd keep as close to that dog as I could and watch for his warnings. That could give you an important few seconds to get into a safe position."

I left and walked the three blocks to the drugstore for the prescription. Daddy was meeting me there after he finished at the sale barn, this being Thursday. As I stood outside the drugstore watching for Daddy, two cars full of high-school kids roared past. Karen and her older brothers, Dan and Harv, were in one car. I raised my arm to wave but they didn't see me.

Slowly my arm came down as though bringing a curtain of isolation with it. Stupid self-pity. I hated myself when these moods came. But there were the doctor's words banging through my head. No driving. It was the first time I'd thought about that. Thirteen now, only a few years away from the wonderful excitement and freedom of driving a car.

But not for me. I was always going to be a passenger, dependent on someone else to haul me around. I wanted to run to Kathryn and cry on her, but she had slammed that door on me with those hard words. "Why not you?"

Daddy's car pulled up then, just ahead of Karen's brothers

61

on their second loop of the town square. This time they saw me and waved, but they didn't stop. I sank in beside Daddy for a silent ride home, feeling like the oldest thirteen-year-old in the world.

I ran into the house to change my clothes so I could help with the evening kennel chores. It had become a routine of ours. But tonight the routine was exploded. Daddy met me at the kennel door with a dog in his arms. It was a young daughter of Pride's, and she was dead.

"Oh no," I wailed. "Which one is it? Becky? Aw, no. Torsion again?"

"Looks like it," he said, biting off his words.

I went up to Champaign for three days over the Christmas holidays. I was excited about going, but as soon as I got to Mom's apartment I wanted to take the next bus home. In my mind the farm was home now.

Mom was all charged up about my visit, though. I could tell it meant a lot to her. She seemed younger and happier than I'd ever seen her. All she talked about was school, the new friends she'd made there, the assistant professor she was dating.

I had the sensation of having been left behind, but oddly enough it didn't bother me. In some unspoken way, I believe we both knew by the end of that vacation that I was permanently planted on the farm with Daddy. Mom was no longer talking about three years from now when we'd be together.

I got back home the day after Christmas, and Daddy and I had our little celebration then. For Daddy I had ordered a book on the history of collies from an ad in a dog magazine. I'd earned the money by helping Kathryn make Christmas decorations for her church's bazaar. She paid me more than the work was worth, but I didn't object because it was the only way I could get money for presents for Mom and Daddy. There had been no allowance since I'd lived here. Daddy didn't seem to think of it.

"I expect money's tight right now," Kathryn had told me once when I mentioned it to her. So I hadn't wanted to ask Daddy for Christmas money.

His present to me was wonderful. It was a grooming coat just like his, only smaller. I'd seen his in the tack bag that he took on show trips. My grooming coat was white nylon, knee length, and on the back was an embroidered collie head with lettering arched above it: "Halsey's Kennels."

Daddy and Baron had been to three more shows in December, and Baron had won or placed well every time. Now he had four points toward the fifteen it took to make him a champion. I wasn't invited on those trips, but several times Daddy had mentioned my going to the big specialty show in January. The grooming coat was a tangible promise that I was now a full-fledged team member.

I relished the days between Christmas and New Year's. With no school I was relieved of the dread that shadowed every school day and increased with the approach of my menstrual periods. Seizures came once a month now, and the law of averages shouted out the fact that they were not all going to happen at night or after school. One of these times, one of these times it was going to happen at school, and that would be it for me.

Karen would stick by me, I was pretty sure. And probably no one would actually throw stones at me or anything like that. I knew the kids at school now; they were basically nice people who wouldn't go out of their way to be cruel. But I knew what the sight of me in full flop was going to do to every one of them, even Karen. No matter how kind or sympathetic they might be, they wouldn't forget that sight.

So the days at home were full of light and freedom for me. Sometimes Karen came over or I went to her house. I spent entire afternoons reading. But the best of the vacation time was spent in the kennel with Daddy.

We were there on New Year's afternoon, working our puppies up and down the alleyway. It was an unusually warm day, warm enough to leave the doors open at the alley ends and let in the sunshine and snow-smelling breeze.

The pups were the two that Daddy had chosen from the pens of adolescent sons and daughters of Pride to take to the specialty show. They were seven-month-old littermates, a dark sable bitch named Elf and a tricolored male named Druid.

Elf was mine to train and groom and show. I'd already spent hours smoothing the sides of her head with a stripping knife to clean out every loose hair. Daddy stood over me and showed me how.

Today we were practicing the pups' gaiting and posing technique and working on my handling skills. Elf moved in a straight line as she was supposed to but wanted to sit down as soon as I stopped instead of walking into a proud, square show stance. Druid would pose beautifully but only for a second or two at a time, and when he gaited he swung his hindquarters to the side. Sidewinding, Daddy called it.

After we'd trotted and posed for half an hour, we hoisted our dogs onto the grooming tables and went to work on them. Daddy had put up a second table for me.

As I began brushing Elf I said, "Turn on the radio, why don't you?"

"What's the matter, your leg tied to a piano?"

I glanced at him, startled. He was looking at me long and deeply, but there was a glimmer at the bottom of it. He was joking with me! I loved it.

I made a face and turned on the radio myself.

As we worked I said, "Are we going to take Pride to the specialty? Did you decide?"

"I'm debating," Daddy said.

"Let's do. Why not?"

"Entry fees, for one thing, girl. Ten dollars a dog, and there's the all-breed show the day after the specialty. If we take Baron and the pups and Pride, that's eighty dollars just in entry fees. We need to take the pups, in hopes of getting them sold. Heck, we've got eleven half-grown collies sitting around here eating their heads off. Got to get some of 'em sold."

"How much do you sell them for? How much does the kennel make, Daddy?"

I was beginning to be interested in the money side of dog breeding because my dream was to stay here all my life and breed dogs with Daddy, and I needed to know whether two people could make enough to live on or whether we'd always have to have outside jobs. Jobs, for me, were going to be a problem. If I couldn't drive to work, if I wouldn't be allowed to work around anything that some people might consider dangerous for me, like machinery, if I wouldn't be allowed to work in a store or office because people might be afraid I'd have a seizure in front of the public . . .

Daddy expanded. "Well, now, young puppies I'll sell for two to three hundred dollars, depending on quality and sex and color. Everybody wants sable bitches, so they bring the most. Older pups, show prospects like these two, they'll bring up around five hundred. Then there's stud fees. A Best in Show winner like Pride, he'll bring in a five-hundred-dollar stud fee from people who own bitches they want to breed to him. So, with our setup here, eight bitches and a Best in Show stud dog, we stand to take in, say, twenty-five, thirty thousand a year."

"Wow." I was safe. I was home free. This was my home and my job both, for the rest of my life.

"Course, you've got to subtract your show expenses and your feed bills and vet bills. Still and all, once I get the loans paid off we should be okay."

"Loans?"

He picked up one of Druid's feet and began nipping off toenail tips.

"Well, I had to borrow a little, you know, to build the kennel and buy the bitches. Sold off my calves a little earlier than I would have otherwise, so they didn't bring quite as much as usual."

I knew that in other years Daddy's pastures had held feeder calves, bought in Missouri in early spring and sold in November after they were grown to butchering size. And I knew that this year there were no calves. The pastures were leased to a neighbor, and so were the hay fields.

He had borrowed money to build the kennel and stock it.

66

He'd counted on selling all those puppies for hundreds of dollars apiece. What if they didn't get sold? What if they kept dying? What happened to his dreams and my future if the kennel failed?

But there was my magnificent Pride, watching us from the first pen, and here were beautiful Elf and Druid, worth hundreds of dollars when the right buyers came along. It was going to be fine.

"Tell you what," Daddy said. "There's a fellow in Louisville that's sending a bitch to be bred to Pride. She ought to be coming in the next few weeks sometime. That'll be five hundred dollars clear profit. If that stud fee comes in before the specialty, we'll buy you some new duds to show in. If you're going to be my assistant handler you've got to look snazzy."

"Like you, in your leather cap?"

"Yep, like me in my cap. We'll get you a tartan plaid wool skirt and a frilly white blouse so you'll look like a Scottish lassie. Hand me that show lead over there."

"What's the matter, your leg tied to a harmonica?" I shot him a sassy look, and we laughed together.

I loved him intensely.

We were eating supper when the phone rang. Daddy talked in monosyllables. "Yeah. No. Well, it's up to you. Thanks for calling."

He slammed the phone down and pounded off into the living room. If he had a colored aura around his body it was bright red right then. I could almost see it myself. Pride, who was in the house every night now, pressed close to me and watched Daddy anxiously.

67

"Who was it?" I asked, leaving the dishes for later.

"Al Hervey, over in Louisville. The one I told you about. He's got a nice champion bitch, and at Danville last fall he said he definitely planned to breed her to Pride. Said she'd be in season right around the first of the year and he'd call me then to make shipping arrangements."

"He changed his mind?" There went the show entries and the new outfit for me.

Daddy glared up at me from his chair. "Damned fool. Said he'd been hearing stories about Pride's offspring dying of torsion. Didn't want to take any chances, he said. Fool."

"But . . ."

I thought of the dogs here that had died, and the one we'd heard about in Indiana, also sired by Pride.

"Does he blame it on Pride?" I asked finally.

Daddy turned away. "Damn fool," he muttered.

Seven

On the last Friday in January Daddy and I drove north toward Hammond, Indiana, and the Illiana Collie Fanciers' specialty show. Mrs. Snorff had given me permission to skip my afternoon classes for the six-hour drive.

Behind us, the station wagon was crammed with four wire crates, two grooming tables, one big suitcase, and various small bags and satchels holding dog food, dishes, and grooming equipment.

Within the wire crates Baron and Pride slept, Elf and Druid lay panting lightly and staring around them. Elf cringed every time a car whooshed past us. Twice already she had thrown up, and we'd had to pull off the road and stop to clean up the mess in her crate.

By five o'clock it was almost dark. We had passed Danville an hour before and were being engulfed by the south Chicago sprawl of towns and traffic. I was intensely excited, going to my first dog show, but Daddy was just tense. He gripped the wheel with both hands and made me check the road map repeatedly to be sure we hadn't passed our turn.

Commuter traffic swelled around our car, slowing us. I'd been hungry for quite a while now, but I knew we had to find Hammond first, find the show building and the hotel and get the dogs unloaded, before we could think about supper.

One good thing, I reminded myself. I'd had my period two weeks ago, with its accompanying grand mal seizure, so I felt reasonably safe for this weekend. I could acknowledge my tension and know that it was nothing more than normal excitement, not the beginning of an aura.

Although Daddy's tension increased as the city traffic packed us in, he'd been withdrawn during the whole trip. He'd been to so many dog shows that I didn't expect him to feel the way I did about this one, but I had expected some excitement, at least a little cheer. We were on our way to an important collie specialty show, we were bringing Pride out of retirement as well as showing off three lovely pups of his, and it would be my first show ever. On top of that, I would actually be showing a dog myself. How could Daddy not be excited?

He was worried about money, I knew. After the Kentucky man had canceled the breeding to Pride, Daddy decided not to spend the entry money for the all-breed dog show the day after the specialty. He also changed our hotel reservations from the expensive hotel where the show was headquartered to a cheaper one across the road. And he picked through my school clothes for a show outfit instead of buying the Scottish things we'd talked about.

It scared me to think that there might not be enough money. I didn't want to be that grown up. Much as I longed to be adult and free, part of me wanted to bury my head in childhood, where other people took care of me and worried about money if they had to but didn't tell me about it.

Still, money worries and seizure worries could both wait until after this weekend. We were almost there!

We found Hammond, found the street we were looking for, and eventually found our cluster of buildings. The show building was a national guard armory on a main thoroughfare. Next door to the armory was the plush hotel where most of the dog-show people would be staying. Across the highway was our smaller, shabbier motel.

We stopped at the motel only long enough to check in, then waited several minutes for a break in the traffic. When it came we lurched across the highway and into the armory parking lot, where several station wagons were gathered around an open double door.

Daddy carried Pride's crate into the building while I led the dog and carried a grooming table. The room we entered was vast, warm, brightly lit. Friendly voices called and laughed and joked. I started smiling uncontrollably.

In the center of the room were three huge show rings with white lattice fencing around them. At each ring entrance stood small tables with bouquets of flowers. Just inside each ring were four plywood figures of collies, each with a large number, one to four, painted on it. Each plywood collie was painted a different collie color: sable, tricolor, blue merle, or white.

Around the outer spaces of the room people were setting up their small individual camps, clusters of wire crates and grooming tables, lawn chairs and ice chests and grocery bags full of snacks. Small children led huge collies in racing romps at the far end of the room, where there was space for stretching travel-cramped legs.

Daddy found an open space for us. As quickly as we could, we unloaded all of our dogs and equipment. Daddy set out dog food dishes on one of the grooming tables and began mixing canned and dried food for our gang. I watched for a chance to help.

A big, hearty young man came by and said, "Hey, Clint. Glad you made it. Who have you got?"

Daddy nodded toward the crates. "That's Pride there. Got him entered in the Stud Dog class. Baron there, I've been showing him some this fall. Son of Pride's. And then the two youngsters over there, they're by Pride, too. This'll be their first time out."

I waited for him to introduce me, but he forgot.

The man, whose badge said Show Chairman, wandered away but called back as he left, "We've got a little buffet supper over there, free for exhibitors, and we'll have coffee and rolls in the morning. Help yourselves."

Daddy said he wasn't hungry and went to move our car away from the loading zone. I guarded the dogs till he came back, but when he waved me toward the buffet I went eagerly. My stomach had been growling for two hours.

The buffet was on a pretty table at the far end of the room, decorated with flowers and collie figurines scattered among the platters of ham sandwiches, crackers and chips and pickles, cookies and brownies and cakes with collies in the icing. I loaded a paper plate, collected a paper cup of punch, and sat down at a long lunch table nearby.

72

As I ate, the table filled with other people: a family, an older woman, and a middle-aged couple. All of them smiled at me as they sat down, then ignored me and went on with private conversations.

"I see the Tartan contingent is here with about twenty entries," one woman said glumly.

"Yep," another answerd. "There goes Best of Breed, Best Opposite, Winners Dog, Winners Bitch . . ."

Everyone laughed ruefully. I guessed the Tartan kennel must be tough competition. I ate silently, waiting for someone to mention Pride. After all, he was a Best in Show winner. He must be competition worth worrying about.

The people around me ate at a leisurely pace, gazing around at the fellow exhibitors who were still arriving, unloading, and setting up.

"There's those people from Iowa, what's their name? I forget. Heck of a nice young couple, anyway. Met them over at Davenport last spring."

"Oh, look. There's Mabel Odlander. Is she still alive?"

Someone laughed. "I don't know. Hard telling from this distance. She's on her feet and moving, anyhow. Do you know, she's still judging. Can't see her hand in front of her face, but she's still judging dog shows. There ought to be mandatory retirement for judges over two hundred years of age."

Laughter.

"There's a pretty puppy," a woman said of a fluffy sable bitch going past with a small boy attached to her leash.

"Mmm," someone else agreed. "Lovely head quality. A little cow-hocked, though."

73

"I see Clint Halsey is here again. That man doesn't know when to quit, does he?"

Indifferent chuckles answered her. I stiffened.

The man said, "I love it when old Halsey shows up. He's so easy to beat."

"Oh, I don't know," the woman said. "Those dogs he started with were junk, of course, but he's come up with one or two decent ones. That Pride dog, he's a little coarse-headed, but he's not a bad dog."

I bristled. Pride was a Best in Show winner. Didn't the stupid woman know that?

"He has a Best in Show, doesn't he?" another woman asked.

"Oh, yeah, he got lucky one time at some little show down South somewhere. One of those flukey bits of luck. Old Halsey never did show him again after that. Knew enough to quit while he was ahead, I expect. I'm surprised to see him here."

"He's got that young dog he's showing now. Baron, I think his name is. He's a decent collie. Better than the old dog, for sure. They've got a couple of young pups entered. I was over looking at them a while ago. Nothing much there, quality-wise."

They ate in silence for a few minutes, then someone said, "You know, I've tried to like that man, and I just can't. He was always such a poor sport when he got beaten."

"And a worse sport when he won," the man added. "After he got that Best in Show he was downright impossible to be around, bragging it up endlessly."

"I heard he's hocked everything he owns, built a big kennel, bought a whole slew of bitches to breed to that dog of his. Gonna get rich on his Best in Show."

They shook their heads and grinned sadly, wisely.

Someone down the table leaned into the conversation. "I hear he's got torsion in his bloodline. I know of two people that have puppies out of that Pride dog, and both of them died of stomach torsion. You heard anything about that?"

Looks were exchanged. I lowered my eyes to my plate so they wouldn't notice me.

The man said doubtfully, "Well, maybe that was just coincidence. Heck, torsion can happen anywhere. I don't know that it's even inherited, is it?"

"The tendency for it sure can be inherited." Another voice joined in from the next table. "It has to do with long bodies. Those Halsey dogs are very long-bodied, and those are the ones that seem to have the torsion problems. More space in there for the stomachs to shift, is my theory. I'd steer clear of buying or breeding in that direction, for sure."

The conversation turned to names I didn't know, and it was too late for me to interrupt and defend Daddy and Pride. I couldn't have, anyway. For years I'd dreaded public seizures so much that I'd bent all my effort toward staying invisible with other people, especially strangers. Now, when I wanted to break out of that mental binding and stand up for my dog and my father, I couldn't do it.

I went back to our crates and stood around awhile, watching Daddy brush Baron's coat backward, tail to head, so he looked like a toasted marshmallow. Carefully I studied the dog's profile, the details of the planes of his head. Was this a top-quality collie, or was Daddy fooling himself?

Occasionally someone walked past and greeted Daddy or paused to look at our dogs, but I couldn't help noticing the groups of friends greeting friends around other people's crates. Women whooped and hugged each other and asked about mutual friends or one another's children. Men called out across the room or slapped each other's shoulders and offered drinks from their private ice chests.

Daddy and I had each other, of course. I offered to brush out the pups or walk them around the room, anything to feel like a full partner in this business.

"Walk Elf around," he said. "She's kinda timid; it'll help her get used to the place."

I had to pull her out of her crate, she was so scared. Talking gently to her, I eased her into a crouching walk away from our crates. She looked awful, slinking along and flattening her ears in fear. I wanted her to be beautiful and impressive, as she was at home. As that little boy's pup had looked prancing past our supper table and earning compliments from strangers.

As we made our way around the room Elf gradually relaxed and wagged the tip of her tail when people stroked her head in passing. I took her into one of the empty show rings, as I'd seen other people doing, and practiced trotting her up and down the rubber-matting paths that circled the ring. With her feet on the nonslip rubber, she relaxed more and trotted out quite nicely, I thought. I wondered if any of those people who had been insulting our dogs was watching and knew that Elf was a Pride daughter.

I took her back to her crate and, with Daddy's permission, took Pride out for a walk around the room. He grinned his ear-flattening grin and leaned against my leg. Then he led me in a circle of the room, his head high and moving from side to side, his tail thrashing with each step. He was magnificent. I could see it; everybody else could surely see it, too.

We came to a row of crates made of varnished wood, with green plaid letters on their sides saying "Tartan Collies." There were eight matching crates, four separate exercise pens with collies standing inside them, and three grooming tables. Two women and a man, all in matching Tartan Collies grooming coats, worked on dogs who stood or lay patiently on the tables.

The woman at the nearest table sensed me watching, turned, and smiled at me and Pride over her shoulder.

"That's a beautiful dog," I said, to be making contact. I hadn't actually looked at the dog.

"This is Centurion," she said with pride in her voice, as though I should recognize the dog's name.

When I didn't respond, she turned and looked again, and smiled more warmly. "Is this your first show? I don't think I know you, do I?"

"No, it's my first show. I'm March Halsey. Clint Halsey's daughter. This is Pride, of course." I tried to say it in the same way she had presented her dog's name to me.

She quit combing then and gave me her full attention. "So this is Pride. Do you mind if I go over him? I've only seen him in the ring."

I motioned her to go ahead, and she bent over Pride, who tried to kiss her. With skillful fingers she probed and smoothed his head, running a thumb over the step-up between his eyes, cupping his ears in her fingertips, lifting his lip to expose his teeth. She buried her hands in his long coat, pressing his ribs and bearing down on his hindquarters and finally pulling his tail through her hand.

When she'd finished, she just smiled carefully, thanked me, and went back to combing her dog.

"He has a Best in Show," I said foolishly.

"I know." Her voice was kind.

"Well?" I demanded something from her.

Slowly she turned and studied my face. "Do you seriously want to learn collies?" she asked in a quiet tone.

I knew what she meant. Did I want to risk listening to insults about Pride, for the sake of increasing my knowledge? Was I going to be another Clint Halsey with mediocre dogs and a poor attitude when they got beaten?

Was I a separate person, or was I just Clinton Halsey's kid?

I looked her in the eye. "Pride is my pet and I love him," I told her. "But I want to learn."

She nodded and let Centurion jump down from his table to stand beside Pride. "Okay then, put your hand here. Feel these bulging bones on the side of Pride's head? Now feel how flat and clean Turie's backskull is. Look at the muzzles. See how Pride's has a sort of caved-in, veiny look to it, and see what a smooth cylinder Turie's is? Now these are fine points we're talking about, March. I'm not saying Pride isn't a good collie, just that he's not a great one."

And the way Daddy bragged about him, to all these other collie people who had dogs just as good if not better . . . I began to understand how these people probably felt about Daddy.

78

Point by point the woman went over both dogs with me, showing me how long Pride's body was, compared to her dog's. I had never seen that before, nor the fine points of head structure.

"But if he's not really all that good, how come he has a Best in Show?" I demanded finally. "If your dog is so much better, how come Pride is the one with the Best in Show?"

Quietly she said, "Well, actually Centurion has seventeen Best in Shows, so far."

I cringed inside.

"Oh. Congratulations. Well, I'd better get back. Thanks for showing me all that stuff."

"March?" she said as she ushered her dog into his crate. "Listen, you don't have to tell me if you don't want, but I've been hearing some rumors about several of Pride's puppies dying of torsion. Is there any truth in that?"

I hesitated so long that she guessed the answer. With genuine compassion on her face she said, "Oh, that's too bad. But if you're smart you'll quit breeding from that line. The problem is only going to get worse."

"Thanks," I said numbly, and walked away. Easy for her to say, quit breeding from that line. She didn't know Pride was all we had to build our futures on, Daddy and I. Our separate private dreams—his of respect from the dog world, mine simply of shelter and security for the rest of my life—those were all we had. If we didn't have Pride and his sons and daughters to build on, we didn't have anything.

Don't think about that now, I told myself harshly. You've been looking forward to this show for months. Don't let anything spoil your fun. Just relax and enjoy it.

Eight

Next morning we breakfasted on the free coffee, juice, and rolls offered to exhibitors by the host collie club.

Daddy explained our day's schedule as we ate. "Puppy Sweepstakes start at nine. I'll show Druid first, in the Puppy Dogs Six to Nine Months Old class, and you'll show Elf in Puppy Bitches Six to Nine. The top two winners in each of the six classes will compete for Best in Sweeps. It's usually a cash prize and a nice big trophy. That'll take all morning. Regular classes will start after lunch. You'll show Elf again in the regular puppy classes, and I'll show Druid and Baron. They'll have dog classes—that is, males— judged in one ring and bitches in the other ring. Then later on, after all the puppy and open classes, we'll show Pride in the Stud Dog class, along with his offspring—Baron, Druid, and Elf. We'll have to find somebody to take Baron and Druid in."

I said, "That's the class where they judge a dog on the quality of the puppies he's produced, right?"

"That's right. And after that will be the specials class, for all the champions going for Best in Show."

"Will Pride have a good chance of winning it?" I asked, wanting to hope.

"Oh, sure. He's got a good chance. He's a Best in Show winner, don't forget."

Silently I said, Yes, and Centurion has won Best in Show seventeen times. We're outclassed, Daddy, and you won't admit it.

Back in the grooming area we put Elf and Druid on the tables and went to work on their coats. Daddy watched over me, but I did all the work on Elf, snipping each whisker stubble down to the skin with small pointed scissors, brushing her whole coat forward and spraying it with water and coat dressing to make it fluff out. I dampened her white feet and neck collar and rubbed them with a block of special grooming chalk to make them dazzling white.

Nine o'clock. I took off my new grooming coat, which was now covered with chalk and collie hair. With nervous movements I brushed my own hair with the brush I'd been using on Elf, slipped her show lead over her head, and eased her onto the floor. Daddy was already at the ring entrance with Druid.

The room was much more crowded today than it had been last night. The crating space around the rings was full of crates and dogs and people, but spirits were high and voices cheerful. I felt intoxicated with the excitement of being part of this world at last. Win or lose, I was having a wonderful time.

The first class of the Puppy Sweeps was called, and Daddy filed into the ring with Druid dancing and pulling against his lead. I maneuvered close to the ring to study the handling procedure, so I'd know what to do when it was my turn. My stomach trembled with nervous anticipation.

There were six gangly adolescent collies in the ring, sables and tricolors and one blue merle. They circled the ring at a trot, then posed while the judge made her way down the line. Squinting, I studied each pup as the judge went over him, and reluctantly decided that at least two of the six were better than Druid, based on what the Tartan woman had shown me last night about head structure.

When the judge announced her placements, Daddy and Druid were sent to stand before the fourth-place marker, and the two I'd chosen were placed first and second. Daddy accepted his white ribbon from the judge in unsmiling silence.

I kept my ringside spot and watched Puppy Dogs Nine to Twelve Months and Puppy Dogs Twelve to Eighteen, trying to guess which dogs the judge would like. I was right both times.

Then finally it was our turn. "Puppy Bitches Six to Nine," the steward called from the ring entrance.

I held back until two others had entered the ring ahead of me. I didn't want to have to lead off, my first time in the ring. When Elf was posed correctly I glanced back to see five more puppy bitches filing into the ring behind me. This was the biggest class yet. Eight dogs and only four placements. We would probably be out of the ribbons, I warned myself.

The judge made a circling motion over her head and sent us around the ring at a fast trot, twice around. It was the most exhilarating moment of my life. Elf moved fast and straight beside me, her head up, tail waving.

We halted and posed. The judge walked to the first pup and made a low whistling sound. The pup hung her head and flattened her ears in shyness, then cringed when the judge ran her hands over her body.

While she examined the second dog in line, I double-checked to be sure that Elf's legs were straight under her and that her head was up. Would she cringe away from the touch of a stranger, too? Maybe.

The judge was at my right shoulder, making her soft whistling sound. Elf's ears pricked into perfect folded-tip alertness; her eyes brightened as they studied the judge.

She tensed at the judge's touch but didn't pull away, and the tip of her tail wagged. After her examination, the judge gave Elf a friendly pat on the rump and threw me a quick smile. I loved her.

When she'd looked all of them over, the judge came back to the first pup and motioned for individual gaiting. The first handler moved her dog across the ring and back. The competitor in me was pleased to see the pup half cringing as she moved. The other half of me felt sorry for the handler, knowing that Elf might do the same.

But when our turn came Elf sailed in fine style across the ring. And later, after the class made a final circle of the ring, I was thrilled but not surprised to find myself standing in front of the second-place collie-shaped marker, receiving from the judge a red ribbon and the murmured words, "That's a nice little bitch. You'll do well with her when she matures."

The rest of the day was long stretches of impatient waiting, broken by bits of intense excitement. There was a wait of almost an hour before the final Puppy Sweepstakes runoff, in which all of the first- and second-place winners came back into the ring for Best in Sweeps. Elf and I worked hard at it, but the four placements went to others.

Then, after a long lunch break, the process began again— puppy classes, then the adult classes. This time there was simultaneous conformation judging in two rings, with obedience classes in the third. Elf and I were in the bitch class at the same time Daddy and Druid were in the dog class. Druid was out of the ribbons; Elf and I won our class. The exhibitors we'd just beaten paused beside me on their way out of the ring to pat my shoulder and say "Congratulations." I glowed and glowed.

Then Daddy switched Druid for Baron, whom we had groomed during the lunch break, and I put Elf away to rest during the long open classes to come.

Baron looked very good to me and showed well, but he did no better than third in his class of four.

Again, long nervous waits through the adult classes— Bred by Exhibitor, American Bred, Open Sable, Open Tri-Color, Open Blue, and Open White. I got Pride out and began grooming him, to make the time pass. Finally, near four o'clock, the open dog classes were finished and the Stud Dog class called.

There were only four entries, but each entry consisted of the stud dog plus at least two of his offspring. Centurion led the way, with seven young dogs and bitches in his wake. Then came Daddy and Pride, with Elf and me, and Baron and Druid handled by two men I didn't know whom Daddy had recruited at the last minute. Two other dog families followed. It took forever for the judge to go over all those dogs, and the outcome was inevitable. Centurion won. Pride came in fourth.

I could see Daddy's head and neck go rigid with anger as we left the ring, but there was no time to say anything. In the next ring they were calling for the Winners Bitch class. Elf and I ran for it.

There were seven in the class, the winners of all of the puppy and open bitch classes. Whoever won now would get five points toward her championship title. One-third of a championship, all at once. I looked up the line and knew Elf wasn't a contender. The open winners were fully mature, long-coated and gorgeous. So I wasn't disappointed when the Open Sable bitch received the fateful finger-point from the judge. I started to congratulate the winner but realized no one else was leaving the ring. Oh, yes. Reserve winners. Daddy had explained about that.

I stayed in the ring while the class circled again and was already mentally out of the ring and back to Daddy when I realized the judge was pointing at me.

Reserve winner? I hesitated, thinking I'd misunderstood his gesture. But I was being congratulated, and there was the huge purple-and-white rosette in my hand and a crystal plate with a collie head etched in its center.

I sailed out of the ring on feet that didn't touch the floor.

As I came out of the ring a young couple stopped me to admire Elf. "She wouldn't be for sale, I don't suppose?" the man said.

Daddy appeared then. "She might be, if you can afford her," he said. He had Pride beside him and one eye on the rings. It was almost time for Best in Show.

The young man ran his hands over Elf's head. "I've been looking for a good young bitch. My wife and I, we've been showing for a year or so, but really our dog is just pet quality. We need something better to breed from. How much are you asking for her?"

"Twelve hundred," Daddy said quickly. "This here is her sire. You've probably heard of him. Champion Halsey's Pride. Best in Show winner. I get top prices for his get."

The man and woman exchanged questioning looks. I held my breath. Twelve hundred dollars was a fortune. If we could sell Pride's daughters for that amount . . .

We were startled by a high squawking noise that set all two hundred collies barking. I turned and saw a man marching toward us, a Scottish bagpipe waving its banners over his shoulder. He wore a short plaid kilt, a black velvet jacket, and a froth of white lace at his neck and wrists.

Daddy gave me a huge grin and said, "Here we go for the specials class. Wish us luck."

Turning toward the rings, I saw that the partition between two rings had been removed to make one huge ring into which the parade was moving. The piper led the way, striding out fast enough to flare the pipe's banners behind him. The tune he played was vaguely familiar, a stirring

86

march that brought tears to my eyes. And behind the piper came thirty-five of the most beautiful collies in the country, all glossy and sparkling and prancing with excitement.

There weren't enough chairs at ringside, so I sat on the floor beside the young couple, and Elf lay between us. I heard the woman whisper to her husband, "We can afford twelve hundred if they'll let us pay half down. Our income tax refund will cover the rest, won't it?"

I rubbed Elf's side, elated. The show was a success. We'd gotten a wonderful placement with Elf and sold her for a huge profit. With my affections centered mainly on Pride, and spread over thirty other dogs, I wouldn't miss this one painfully. The important thing was that Daddy would feel so good about the sale, and even more important, we were making a living as dog breeders. I could do this all my life, with Daddy, and be safe!

The young woman beside me played with Elf's head, stroking it and talking baby talk until Elf thrashed her tail and wriggled onto her back for a tummy rub. She'd be going to a good home, I could tell. I grinned at the woman.

Her husband said, "This class will take at least an hour. Want a Coke, popcorn?" He included me in the question and I nodded eagerly. I was starved.

He was gone a long time. I glanced over toward the concession booth once and saw him in conversation with a woman who was shaking her head emphatically and looking toward us.

Oh no, I thought.

He came back, deposited a Coke and a popcorn bag with me, and said, "Come on, honey, over here a minute."

87

They didn't come back. I sat through the long Specials class hoping I was wrong. When Centurion leaped to the applause of the big win, I clapped, too, knowing he deserved it more than my darling Pride did. And knowing, too, that we'd lost the sale.

Daddy said little as we began packing our equipment. Just as we were ready to take the first load to the car, the young couple came back.

Hope rose in me but died when I saw the embarrassed expression on the woman's face.

"We changed our mind about buying the puppy," the man said to Daddy. "I'll be honest with you. I've heard from a couple of different people that you've got a lot of torsion in your bloodline. They said half a dozen of Pride's offspring have died of it. We just can't take that chance. We don't have that kind of money to gamble on a bitch that might drop dead any minute. I'm sorry."

I ached for them and for us, for the truth of what he said. But Daddy turned almost viciously and said, "It ain't true. Not a word of it. It's a smear campaign against me and my dogs, because we beat too many people. They got jealous and started rumors, and that's all it is. I don't care. Keep your damned money. You'll never find another bitch this good, not for that price. I know what I've got here, even if you're too stupid to."

"Daddy—"

"Shut up and get these crates over to the door. I'll go drive the car up where we can load."

He stamped away, hunched in his anger.

I turned to the couple and tried to smile a little. "Don't

mind him," I said. "He loves his dogs so much, he just takes everything too hard. Too personal."

They turned and left without a word, but the woman touched my arm as she went.

It was an endless, wordless drive home. We picked up hamburgers to go at the edge of the city, then drove steadily south, hour after hour. I folded my jacket against the car door for a pillow and dozed or pretended to doze most of the way. I didn't want to talk to Daddy, and he obviously was in no mood for happy chatter either.

I tried to concentrate on remembering the thrill of Elf's wins, the kindness of the people I'd talked to last night and today. Those were good, golden, warming thoughts, but they couldn't entirely block out the dark dread that our collie kennel was going to fail. It would fail not because our dogs weren't good enough—today's comparisons reassured me that there were many others worse than ours. It would fail because Pride carried a bad gene. Somehow, his puppies inherited from him a fatal weakness.

I knew, I *knew* that I must face this fact and come to terms with it. Daddy could not, so I must.

But I didn't know how.

Nine

February was a dreary month for Daddy and me. The days were overcast and chilly, with drizzling rain washing away the last of the snow, then freezing into sheets of ice. Walking from the house to the kennel was an athletic challenge. Dog droppings froze solid in the runs and had to be chipped up with the spade.

Daddy and Baron went alone to a show in St. Louis, and Baron was out of the ribbons. The next weekend was a local show at Carbondale, so I got to go along. We won that day, but the entry was small. The win was worth only one championship point, bringing Baron's total to five. Ten more to go.

The next weekend we stayed home, and Daddy ran ads in all the local papers, trying to sell some puppies. We'd only sold two all month, and we'd had twenty-three new puppies born. Several people called in answer to the ad, but the weather was bad and the roads icy. Only one family arrived. They wanted Elf; Daddy wanted eight hundred dollars for her. They couldn't afford more than two hundred, they said, and in the end Daddy let her go.

I hated it all. How could we hope to make a living breeding dogs when the puppies didn't get sold, our best-quality stock only brought a fraction of its worth, and the unsold dogs went on eating?

"It's a smear campaign," Daddy snarled when I tried to talk to him about Elf's sale. "Those damn show breeders are spreading these stories about Pride, just to get me. A bitch like Elf is worth every bit of twelve hundred to a show breeder. She's got the wins to prove it. Reserve at the Illiana specialty, that's a solid, brag-dog win. Two hundred dollars for a bitch like that. It's a damn crime."

Once when he was out I looked through the papers on his desk and found a past-due statement from the dog-food company, saying they'd have to close his account if he didn't pay the outstanding balance within thirty days. The next time we got dog food it was delivered from the local feed mill, and it wasn't as good. The dogs tried to bury their feed pans instead of eating the food in them.

But if home was dreary those weeks, school was gradually becoming the bright part of my life. The fact amazed me. Back in Champaign school had been something to be endured every day until the three o'clock bell set me free. I'd been one of the invisible kids in that school, the kind of student that even the teachers seemed to have trouble recognizing and remembering.

The Coalville school was so tiny, so unthreatening, that it

seemed almost like an expanded family. I was dragged into projects so quickly that I had no time to hang back. I ran a booth at the fun fair. I was shoved into the job of assistant equipment manager for the girls' basketball team, a job that would carry over to softball and track in the spring, they assured me. And I was assigned a part in the seventh-grade class play.

Everyone was in the play, so having a part was no distinction, but it excited me anyway. The play was written by a Coalville graduate who had dreams of becoming a playwright, so it was perfect for our class. It was called *Fast Track*, and it was about a high-school track star in a small town in southern Illinois, obviously Coalville. In the play, the boy had to choose between cheating in the big race and destroying his best friend, and since he was a very honest athlete hoping for a college scholarship it was a terrible decision for him.

Bob Lomar, who was the tallest and best-looking of the five boys in class, played the lead. Karen played his understanding girlfriend and I, because of my mature face and voice, played his mother. It wasn't one of the starring roles by any means, but it had quite a few lines and some good dramatic scenes, and I was proud of it.

Since most of the cast had basketball practice after school, the teachers let us do our rehearsing during class time, the last period each afternoon. In the early stages of rehearsal groups just gathered in separate corners of the classroom and read our parts aloud, but during the last two weeks of rehearsals we shifted to the stage at the end of the gym.

Thursday night was dress rehearsal in the gym; performances would be Friday and Saturday nights. The whole town turned out for class plays, I was told. Nothing much else to do in a town this size.

On Thursday night I rode into town with Karen and her mother. Karen wore her first-act clothes, which were ordinary jeans and a shirt, but I was in my mother costume, a print housedress, an apron, and ugly shoes, all borrowed from Kathryn. I had rubbed Vaseline into my hair and powdered it with flour and drawn lines at the corners of my eyes and around my mouth to age my face. Our production had no one in charge of costumes or makeup, so we were all on our own in those departments.

I'd been experimenting all week with the hair and makeup, standing far back from the mirror to see if the effect would carry to the audience. I was perfect as a forty-year-old woman.

Mrs. Granson, the English teacher, was our director. She motioned Bob and me into our positions, then waved for silence.

"Okay, kids, this is a complete run-through, just like an actual performance. If you flub a line you'll have to fake it and go on as best you can. You won't be able to stop and get help. But you all know your lines by now, and you shouldn't have any trouble. Okay. The audience is seated and waiting. The lights are dark back here. When I give the signal the music will start. Stage lights will come up, and then the curtain. Got that?

"March, remember not to look at the audience. Keep your eyes on Bob, but listen for the curtain to finish opening. If there's applause, wait till it dies down completely before you start to speak, or the audience will miss your opening line."

I nodded. I was standing near the stage fireplace. The scene was a living room, and Bob was sprawled on the sofa. All through rehearsals he'd been loose and full of jokes, but tonight his sprawl had a rigidity that exposed his stage fright. Surprisingly, I wasn't nervous at all, now that it was about to begin. I knew my lines and my stage moves better than any of the others, because I'd memorized so intensely. My old study habits were paying off now, I realized.

With two sharp claps from Mrs. Granson's hands, all talking ceased. Houselights dimmed in the gym. Recorded music rose from the sound system. Our living room was flooded with the glare of footlights.

I drew in my breath. A slight dizziness stirred my brain. Excitement, that was all it was.

With a swoosh and small clatter the curtain swept open.

"Applause, applause!" Mrs. Granson shouted as she clapped.

I smiled my motherly smile at Bob and poised, waiting. The applause ended.

"It's four o'clock, son. Aren't you late for track practice?"

As I listened to his answer I congratulated myself on getting past the "track practice" tongue twister.

I took my three steps toward him, saying the next line. A feeling of panic came into my head. Stage fright, that was all. It was *not* . . . Of course I had, in practice. It couldn't be . . . no.

Oh, God, please no.

The awful stench was in my nose and mouth. The dark cloud of senseless terror flew toward my face and my numb arms couldn't lift to fend it off. I stretched out my hand, trying to lower myself to the floor, but already my arms and legs were rigid. I saw Bob's arm and face as he reached toward me.

Then I disappeared.

When I woke up it was late afternoon. Pride was on the bed beside me, and Kathryn was reading in the living room, just beyond my bedroom door. She heard me stirring and came in to sit on the foot of the bed with Pride.

I looked at her and tried to say something, but I was too miserable for words. Tears streamed down my face. I sat up and held out my arms, and she moved into them. She held me and stroked my back, my greasy, floury hair. After a few minutes she patted me briskly and set me away from her.

"How do you feel?" she asked, studying my face. "How's your tongue this time?"

I opened my mouth and tried moving things. The tongue was fine, but I'd bitten a chunk out of the inside of my cheek. It felt and tasted like raw meat and it hurt like fury when my tongue touched it.

I pointed to it and sniffled.

"Nothing we can do about that," Kathryn said cheerfully. "Time will heal it."

Two thoughts swamped my mind. In just a few hours the play would begin, with or without me. And whether or not I went ahead with the play, I was going to have to face those people again. All those kids. The entire seventh grade, plus

Mrs. Granson. They'd seen me fall down in a staring-eyed faint. They'd seen my body stiffen, then jerk about on the floor uncontrollably.

They'd seen bloody foam coming out of my mouth and a shameful spread of urine wetting my skirt.

I couldn't go back and face them. I absolutely couldn't. My terror at the idea must have been plain on my face, because Kathryn drew away from me slightly, and the concern in her face cooled to something else. I couldn't read her expression.

To my unspoken anguished "Why me?" she was saying again with her eyes, "Why not you?"

The phone rang, shattering the brittle air between us. Pride jumped off the bed to follow Kathryn into the other room. I listened.

"She's just now waking up. . . . I'm not sure. . . . No, she has epilepsy. It was just an ordinary seizure, nothing to be alarmed about. . . . Well, I'm not sure about that. Let me ask her. Hold on."

She came to the doorway and stood large within its frame. "It's Mrs. Granson, calling to find out if you're going to be okay by play time, or should she have the understudy take your part?"

I lay back and took inventory. I was still sluggish with the unnatural need for sleep that always followed a seizure. All my muscles ached, arms and legs and neck and chest and stomach. Even my toes ached when I bent them upward to test things.

"Testing testing one two three," I said. The bitten inner cheek felt so swollen that it seemed to fill my whole mouth, making mush of the words.

I shook my head.

Kathryn stared at me for a moment, weighing my disability claim. Then, still expressionless, she returned to the telephone and said, "Better use the understudy, tonight anyway. Maybe by tomorrow. . . . I'll tell her. Thanks for calling."

"Everybody at school sends their best wishes," she said, coming back into my room. "They hope you'll be able to do the play tomorrow night."

"Me, too."

She studied me, trying to see if I meant it.

Thickly I said, "You don't need to stay. Thanks for being here, though. Daddy'll be home pretty soon. I'll be okay."

"I'm not so sure about that," Kathryn said gruffly. "You just go back to sleep if you want, and I'll read a while more till your daddy gets home."

As my head sank back into the pillow I wondered what she meant when she said, "I'm not so sure." What more could happen to me at this point? The worst possible thing had already happened, and I was going to have to face its repercussions soon.

I closed my eyes and pictured what was going to happen. I'd go to school tomorrow night to do my part in the play, and everyone would stare at me, seeing again in their minds the horror that they'd witnessed before.

They'd speak to me, ask me if I was feeling okay, but they'd get away from me as fast as they could. They'd begin finding ways to avoid me after this.

Silently I wept for the old anonymity of the big school at Champaign. If this had happened there it would have been terrible, but for it to happen in a school where everyone

97

from the principal to the janitor knew me by name and liked me . . . My mind couldn't stretch over the awfulness of facing them.

Like a shy dog my thoughts twisted to the side, back and forth, looking for a way out. Go back and live with Mom? Cowardly. Everyone here would know why I was running away. Karen would despise me for it. She'd shrug me out of her life. Her big brother, Dan, on whom I had a secret crush, would forget me in a week—except to remember the stories he heard at school about my fit.

And going back to Mom would mean giving up the dogs. Pride. The dream of living here forever as a dog breeder. Impractical as that dream might seem right now, it was still the most wonderful thing to come into my life, and I couldn't walk away from it.

Stay here with Daddy but quit school? He'd never let me, and neither would the law, at least till I was sixteen.

Then I would have to stay and face it at school.

Or kill myself.

The thought was startling, but it wasn't a stranger to me. It came peeking into my head like a small serpent whenever I was most depressed about my condition, my future. There had been times when I knew I couldn't face much more, and the dream of death was powerful. But I'd never taken it seriously, never pondered ways and means.

Not until now.

If Kathryn would only go home, I could do it right now before I lost my nerve. I could get up, go into the bathroom, find something in there, some pills or Daddy's razor blades or something. Then it would be all over. I wouldn't have to go back to that school ever again.

Into my head came the dogs. Pride, who was now asleep again along my side. In a flash vision I saw myself in the dog-show ring accepting the purple ribbon with Elf and soaring in my spirit. Another flash and I was in the river with Karen, laughing and blowing water and learning to swim.

So I'd had some good moments in my life. Okay. Fine. Time to end it now. Time to kill this thing that made life unbearable. If only Kathryn would leave me alone. . . .

I drifted off to sleep.

Ten

With a full day of sleep behind me I woke, sharply alert, at two in the morning. I had a dim memory of Daddy coming home from work earlier that evening and talking with Kathryn in the kitchen, but nothing after that.

I'd fallen asleep dreaming of the escape of death, and that longing came back to me now. It would take one moment of courage, and then nothing more. No more courage would be demanded of me ever again. No school to face, no years of adult life marred by the fear of seizures, by the seizures themselves.

Just get out of bed, walk into the bathroom, find Daddy's razor blades. Pain for a little while, then the bliss of endless sleep.

Over and over in my mind I rehearsed the movements: legs over the side of the bed, stand up, walk across the bed-room . . .

Almost without conscious effort the movements replaced the thought of them, and I was across the room, in the hallway.

A rustling from the living room startled me. Kathryn rose from the chair and tottered toward me, her hair and clothes rumpled, her breath sour with sleep.

"Where are you going?" she asked in a harsh whisper.

"Bathroom."

She stared long and hard at me.

"I have to go to the bathroom," I repeated, and moved past her. I shut the bathroom door and sat down on the toilet. Impossible to go through with it now, with Kathryn listening just beyond the partition. I could hear her breathing, and surely she could hear my noises.

I sat for a long time, but there was nothing to be done. Finally I got up, flushed, and opened the door.

She followed me back to my room and sat on the corner of my bed.

"How come you're still here?" I asked as I pulled the sheet up over my legs. It wasn't unusual to wake from a seizure sleep and find her there with me, but never before had she stayed on after I woke.

"Just keeping an eye on you," she said.

Outdoors a full moon rode low in the sky, its glow outlining my bed and dresser and the woman who sat watching me. It etched her face but left her eyes invisible within their shadowed sockets.

"Why?"

"Don't want anything to happen to you," she said curtly.

"What makes you think—"

"You had a look on your face last night, girl. I've seen that look before, and I'm not likely to forget it in my life-time."

"What look? Who—"

"Your uncle Ted," she said flatly.

I waited for her to go on. After a while she seemed to come to a decision. She pulled in a long breath and said, "Ted didn't just die, March. He took his daddy's shotgun and killed himself. And he killed a good deal more than that while he was at it. He killed a big part of my life, and your daddy's, too."

I sat immobile, waiting, dreading to hear this.

"See, March, we were more than just friends, the three of us. I was in love with Teddy by the time I was twelve. Course, no one took it seriously, a little old shirttail girl like I was. Teddy maybe never even knew it, I'm not sure. But I knew it, all the way down to my toes. He was my natural mate, and with him gone there wasn't any hope for husband or children, not for me.

"And your daddy, he was never the same after it happened either. He never did get over feeling guilty about Ted. Teddy was his big brother and Clint loved him, but he hated him, too, because of the seizures. Back then there were still a lot of ignorant people around here, who thought people who had epilepsy were crazy people who ought to be locked up. The Halsey family tried their best to keep Ted's condition a secret. My daddy was his doctor, and I was his constant companion, so Clint and I knew about it, but not many people outside the family knew it.

"Then this one day when Ted was fifteen and I was about

102

your age, he had a seizure out there in the yard in front of three of his friends from school. The boys were all pretty upset by it. One boy even threw up. It wasn't a real deep seizure; I don't think Ted was even completely unconscious. Anyway, when it was over and he could walk again, he went inside the house and came out again carrying that shotgun. I just kind of froze in place, watching him walk up the hill into the orchard. Then I took off running after him, to try to stop him. I remember I looked back over my shoulder to yell at Clinton to come help, and he was standing there with a look on his face I'll never forget. For that one split second he knew what Ted was going to do, and he made his decision not to stop it.

"Then he came running after me and we followed Ted, but not fast enough."

The room was very still, so still that I thought her last words would never stop echoing on the air.

"You thought that was what I was going to do?" I said finally.

Her head tilted back until she was studying me down the length of her broad nose. "I don't know, and I'm not asking. I think you've got more courage than Ted did, courage enough to face what you have to and get on with your life. But I'm not sure. Did you think about what I said, that day you said, 'Why me?'"

"You said, 'Why not you?' I thought it was the cruelest thing a person could say."

"But have you thought about it?"

I sat silent, unwilling to answer.

"What did you think I meant by it?" she insisted.

103

I shrugged and turned my head aside. "I guess, that bad things happen to lots of people, so why should I expect to be any different."

She grunted softly. "You've got the meaning, but you haven't absorbed the logic of it yet. You will, someday, and when you do, it'll make things easier for you."

She rose then and squeezed my ankle through the blanket. I heard her go out the front door, closing it softly behind her. Kneeling on the bed, I watched her cross the yard and move up the road toward her own house, carrying with her a store of wisdom and strength that I needed so much and despaired of.

In the brightly lit parlor I said to my son, "It's four o'clock. Shouldn't you be going to track practice?"

The glare of footlights blinded me to the faces in the audience beyond, but I knew Daddy and Kathryn were there, second row on the aisle. I'd peeked out before the curtain went up, along with the rest of the cast searching for parents.

Mrs. Granson had been relieved to have me back, but she was so busy with details that nothing was said about my seizure, by her or by the kids. They looked at me from the corners of their eyes but said only, "Glad you're feeling better." They were engrossed in their own battles with stage fright and lines of dialogue that disappeared from their memories.

My mouth was sore, but if I spoke carefully I could project the words as clearly as ever, aiming my voice toward the far end of the gym as Mrs. Granson had instructed us to do.

104

When it was all over, Karen pulled me into the line of stars, in the front row, for the six curtain-call bows. Her hand held mine so tightly the bones crunched. My victory was hers, too, she told me with that grip.

The play and the intervening Sunday were helpful, but by Monday morning I was stiff with dread about going to school.

I took my usual seat on the bus beside Karen, and we talked about the play all the way into town. She was tense, too. I could hear it in her voice. But when our eyes met I saw compassion and support in hers, not the repulsion I dreaded. Nothing was said about my seizure. I knew she had checked on me Friday after school, while I was still sleeping it off, and she'd called on Saturday morning to see if I'd be doing the play. She'd wanted to come by Saturday afternoon, but I'd told her I was still resting. She'd called again on Sunday, but again I invented excuses. If I had seen in her eyes the end of our friendship, I might have been tempted back into the dream of death. I didn't trust myself or her.

But now on the bus everything seemed normal between us. We laughed at the stiff way Bob had delivered his lines, after weeks of bragging that he was immune to stage fright. Karen told me in detail how awful the understudy had been, playing my part, and how terrific I had been on Saturday night. Karen herself had done a near-professional acting job, so it was easy to return her compliments wholeheartedly.

By the time we jumped down from the bus in the school

yard I was feeling almost strong inside. Karen and Kathryn were solidly on my side, and that was the important part.

Daddy was, too. I knew that, from the way he had treated me all weekend. I couldn't tell whether he, like Kathryn, had sensed a crisis passing or whether Kathryn might have said something to him. At any rate, he went out of his way that weekend to be thoughtful and cheerful with me. We'd spent most of Sunday sorting through the three litters of weaning-age puppies, deciding which ones were keepers, which were pet quality, and which should go to show homes. No mention was made of the scarcity of buyers for Halsey collies.

It was Daddy's way of showing love, I felt. He couldn't say the words, but he was trying.

When Karen and I walked up the school steps, Mrs. Snorff was standing just inside the door, watching. Often she stood there as the buses arrived, like a mother counting her children.

She said nothing to me, but she gave me an intensely compassionate look, then smiled her wonderful warm smile as though she liked what she read in my face. Her hand rested for an instant on my shoulder as I moved past in the river of bodies.

Still, I was tense about going into my first class, which was English with Mrs. Granson. I delayed as long as I could, at my locker and in the girls' room, so that the last bell was ringing when I pulled open the classroom door and walked in.

Talking ceased; a heavy hush fell as eyes followed me and pretended not to. My toe caught on the leg of a chair and I almost fell.

106

In an agony of clumsiness I shuffled notebooks and text-books, dropping one with a loud spank.

Mrs. Granson started the class by calling for the reading of our weekend assignment, a one-paragraph description of someone we knew well, focusing on character rather than physical description.

One by one they stood to read their papers, but their eyes were on me. Attention wandered, even among those who were doing the readings.

"March?"

I pulled my paper out and stood to read, thankful for my habit of doing assignments far ahead of time. On such a weekend I'd never have been able to concentrate on this one.

As I stood and turned to face the class, I caught a flash of action from the back row. Jerry Hildebrand, the class clown, was making a crazy face and flapping his hands and arms.

It was me he was mimicking. Me in a seizure.

Suddenly I didn't feel shamed, I felt mad. Plain old mad. This stupid condition wasn't my fault. It just was not my fault, none of it, and I was sick and tired of slinking around hating myself and being afraid to face people.

"Mrs. Granson," I said in a clear voice, "I have my assignment here, but would it be all right if I talked about something else first? I want to explain about what happened to me at dress rehearsal. May I do that?" My voice was strong and clear and proud. I hardly recognized it, but I loved the steel that was holding me up.

Mrs. Granson looked mildly startled, but she said, "Yes, March. That might be a good idea. I'm sure it would be good for all of us to understand more about epilepsy. Please do explain."

I walked to the front of the room and turned to face them. Karen was lying back in her chair, grinning at me just as though she'd known I was going to do this.

I pulled in a deep breath. "What happened the other night at rehearsal is called a grand mal seizure. It's a form of epileptic seizure, and it's caused by something like an electrical short circuit in the brain. I don't understand exactly what causes it, but my doctor says it has to do with electrical activity in the brain and it's something like a surge of extra power."

A girl in the front row tentatively raised her hand. I said, "Terri?"

"What does it feel like when it happens?"

I began to relax then, to talk with my friends rather than to give a speech. "First I get what they call an aura. A little dizziness, and sometimes a feeling that I've been in exactly this same time and place before. Déjà vu, they call it. My doctor says it's because the physical image of what I'm seeing gets to my brain a split second before the thinking part of seeing gets to my brain, so I perceive it as a memory rather than as something I'm seeing for the first time. I don't understand that part of it, but it's a weird feeling.

"Then usually two things happen at the same time. I get a horrible smell in my nose and mouth. That's supposed to be because this electrical surge is in the part of the brain that has to do with senses, and it distorts my sense of smell. But anyway, it smells like . . . a heap of rotting dead elephants in the hot sun."

They laughed at that, wilder laughter than the joke merited, but it served to drain off some nervousness.

"Then along with this horrible smell I get a feeling of just awful terror. I can't explain it. I know it's imaginary, but it's the worst thing I've ever known, and it always comes when a seizure is starting. Then my whole body starts going stiff. I can feel the beginning of that part of it, but then I lose consciousness. I'm completely out during the worst part, at least the part that looks the worst to people around me when it happens. I wake up in a couple of minutes when the seizure is over, but then I get terribly sleepy and I hardly know who or where I am, until I can sleep it off for about a day. After that, I have really sore muscles all over, for three or four days, and lots of times I bite my tongue or the inside of my mouth, and that hurts like crazy for a long time afterward. It's because my jaw muscles clamp down, like all the other muscles, and if my tongue or cheek happens to be in the way, tough luck."

Another girl raised her hand and said, "What about the . . ." She couldn't say the words but motioned around her mouth.

"The foaming at the mouth?" I managed a small smile. "All that is is extra saliva that gets produced during a seizure; I don't know why. It looks bubbly because of the air passing through it when I breathe, and if I've bitten myself it'll have blood in it. That's all that is. It doesn't mean I have rabies or I'm crazy or anything like that. One other thing," I tightened myself for this one. "Sometimes there is involuntary urinating during a seizure because all the muscles are clamping down, including the ones around the bladder."

Two boys near the back made whispered giggling sounds, but Mrs. Granson stabbed them with her eyes.

More questions came then, with gathering speed. How often did I have these seizures? how long had I been having them? how did I catch epilepsy? could people catch it from one another?

"Absolutely not," I said. "It's something that can happen to anyone, and some kids who have it might outgrow it. I'm hoping to, naturally."

We talked on until the end of the period. Some of their interest was probably faked for the sake of delaying the schoolwork, but I didn't care. I could tell that by the time the bell rang everyone in that room knew as much as they wanted to know about epilepsy, that the excitement of my seizure was dispelled by their new knowledge, and that their minds were already turned to their own lives and interests.

I went on to my next class feeling exhilarated. I had won a victory so large that even I couldn't comprehend it.

Eleven

As spring moved toward summer it became increasingly clear that Daddy and I were in financial trouble and that Daddy wasn't facing it.

One Saturday when we went grocery shopping at the big store in Carbondale, Daddy yelled at me for loading the cart with cheap things like crackers and the fatty kind of hamburger. He threw the hamburger back into the meat case and slammed a package of sirloin steaks into the basket in its place.

"We ain't starving yet," he shouted, and took the cart away from me. When we got to the checkout counter he'd filled the cart with every expensive thing he saw, more than a hundred dollars' worth. He only had seventeen dollars in his wallet, so we had to replace most of what he'd taken.

The dogs were now eating the cheapest dog food he could buy, and it showed in their condition. Coats were dull and shedding in clouds, and I could feel hipbones and ribs where flesh had been before. The dogs all ate huge amounts of the new cheap food, trying to get the nutrition they needed, but most of the food passed through their systems without nourishing.

Baron was no longer winning in the show ring. His coat had lost its bloom, and as the flesh melted from his head it took on a gaunt, ugly quality. The veins of his foreface stood clearly visible now that the flesh was shrinking.

It broke my heart to watch the dogs going downhill. Pride was in better shape than the others because he got scraps from my plate at mealtime, but even he was losing coat and weight.

By April Daddy was canceling show entries. "Dogs go out of coat in the spring, that's all," he told me gruffly. "No point showing them when they're not in full coat."

A few of the younger, cuter puppies were sold, but none brought more than a hundred dollars, and it wasn't enough. Daddy began getting notices from the bank about overdue mortgage payments. He threw them away, but I got them out of the wastebasket and read them, and I knew we were in trouble.

To Kathryn I said, "Why won't he just get a full-time job somewhere, so he can make the mortgage payments? Doesn't he know we might lose the farm and have to sell all the dogs and move somewhere else?" It loomed so terrible in my mind that I didn't understand Daddy's blindness to it.

"Reality never was one of Clinton's strong points," Kathryn said dryly. "He'll wake up to it one of these days, I expect."

"But maybe not till it's too late," I wailed.

She gave me a long, level look and went on with her ironing. What I was afraid of might actually happen. She knew it as well as I did.

On the first morning of summer vacation I woke early and got out of bed. I'd intended to be lazy, that first morning of freedom, but I wanted to be lazy with Pride in bed with me. Lately he'd been sleeping in the kennel because his coat was shedding in huge clumps and covering my blanket with long, black dog hairs. I didn't mind it myself, but it made extra work for Kathryn.

Now that summer vacation was here, I'd announced to both Daddy and Kathryn that I was taking over all of the housework and cooking. Just the night before, I'd told Kathryn that I wanted to do all the work myself, if she didn't need the money Daddy was paying her.

"Paying me?" She raised her eyebrows humorously.

"Doesn't he?"

"Lord, no, girl. I've got plenty of money. I don't hire out to keep house for other people. I just take care of your daddy because . . . well, I guess I just always have, all our lives. He needs taking care of, so I've done for him ever since your mama moved out. Habit, I guess."

"Oh." I thought for a while, then said, "Well, I think I should take care of him myself, at least during summer vacation, if you don't mind. I'm not old enough to get a job and earn money, except baby-sitting sometimes. I feel like I should be pulling my weight with the work, even if it doesn't save us any money. Maybe you could come over on your regular day, if you want to, and teach me to cook. Okay?"

113

We agreed on that.

The sun was barely up, but already the dew was drying on the grass, and my thin cotton pajamas were plenty warm enough. I ran barefoot toward the kennel, exhilarated by the cool blue shadows of the sunrise hour. Later on it was going to be hot, but for now it was perfect.

I opened the kennel door, then paused, sensing something wrong. Pride looked at me through his pen door, then quietly turned his head toward the pen next to his.

Already I knew.

Baron lay bloated and dead within his pen.

Aw, no. Not Baron.

I turned toward the door to get Daddy, but he was already there, his gaunt shape black in the doorway with the sun's rays gilding it from behind.

"Baron," I said.

He stood motionless.

I moved toward him, but his rigidity stopped me.

Suddenly he turned and ran toward the house. I didn't follow. It was Pride I needed just then, not Daddy. I opened Pride's pen door and went in.

I was kneeling beside him, crying into his neck, when Daddy reappeared.

"Get away from that dog," he said in a voice without inflection.

I looked up, startled. In his hands was a shotgun.

"Daddy. No!"

"Get away from that dog," he said again, shouting this time.

"Daddy, it's Pride. Don't shoot him. It's not his fault. It's *Pride*, Daddy."

114

He came into the pen and threw me aside. The dog scrambled after me out the kennel door.

I turned and Daddy was in the doorway, the shotgun raised and following Pride. Without knowing what I was doing, I flung myself in front of the dog, my arms spread wide.

A fury I'd never known swept over me. "Why don't you shoot me, too, Daddy? I'm not perfect either, so you might as well shoot both of us."

"Get out of the way, girl."

"No. I won't."

I stared, transfixed, at the black hole of the gun's barrel.

Pride moved away from me to circle back toward the safety of his kennel. The gun barrel followed him. He didn't understand his danger, he only knew something was wrong.

The gun exploded. Pride yelped and fled toward the house. I didn't see where he went; I couldn't take my eyes away from Daddy.

He lowered the gun slowly, and his face crumpled, wet with tears. When I went to him he dropped the gun to the ground and clamped me to him. It wasn't a hug, it was a spasm of need more terrible than any I could imagine. His arms locked like iron around my ribs.

We stood that way for several minutes. Then it was over. He turned away from me and went into the kennel.

Twelve

Summer twilight, blue haze over grass and trees, the rasp of insect song.

As the woman's story came to an end, Dick and Diane Peterson stirred in their lawn chairs. The twilight was almost night by now, and there were four of them seated around the hibachi. March Goodman's husband, Dan, had joined the group silently and had listened to his wife without interrupting her.

The old man with his brag-dog photograph was still across the camping area near the show rings, talking to strangers there, showing his picture.

When it seemed that March was finished talking, Diane said, "Don't leave us hanging there. What happened after that? Was the dog killed when he shot him? Did you lose the farm? Are you Karen's brother?" The last question was aimed at the big, good-natured man who sat with his arm around March.

116

He grinned and nodded, but left the talking to his wife.

"No, Pride wasn't badly hurt. He ran out into the road just as Kathryn was driving by, and she took him into town to the vet. He'd picked up a little of the shot in his hip, but it wasn't bad.

"Daddy seemed to fall completely apart, though, over Baron dying of torsion like all the others. For a while he was a crazy man, drinking hard every day, although he'd never been a drinker before. I moved over to Kathryn's house, me and Pride, and I took over the kennel chores at home. After a while Daddy went off, just left without saying anything to anyone. But then he wrote to me from North Dakota. He was working with a custom threshing crew up there, making money in the wheat harvest.

"He was away about three years, working with one kind of traveling crew or another, sending money home for the mortgage payments and for my expenses. I stayed on with Kathryn, all through high school."

March and Dan leaned closer together and held hands. Shared memories bound them.

"What about the kennel?" Dick Peterson asked.

"I ran it. With Daddy sending money home again, I got the dogs back on good food, sold most of the puppies, but kept a few of the really good bitches. Then I started going to dog shows on my own with Dan. Began to learn what I needed to know, bred my bitches to top dogs from other bloodlines, and gradually built my own line again from scratch, without the bad genes from Pride. When I got out of high school I opened the kennel for boarding, learned to do some pet grooming, made it into a paying business. Dan

117

helped me a lot. I started getting into professional handling with his help, and that paid off well. I never did outgrow the epilepsy, and the medication never has dependably controlled the seizures for me, so I haven't been able to get a driver's license. I couldn't have gone into handling without Dan to drive for me."

Diane said, "What happened to Pride, and your father?"

Calmly March said, "Pride did die of torsion, but not until he was thirteen years old. He was our house pet all his life. Kathryn died just a couple of years after Dan and I got married, and she left her house to Dan and me. We still have it, and the kennel.

"Daddy came back home around then, too, and just went back to living in the old home place. Worked at odd jobs around the area, part-time at the sale barn, and things like that. But for years he ignored the kennel totally. Wouldn't even look at the building. It's just the last few years that he's started going with us on some of our show trips. He carries that picture of Pride in his wallet and brags him up to anyone who will listen to him."

The four of them were silent, listening to the chirr of insects and the voices of other dog-show people sitting beside their rigs.

"Funny," Diane said thoughtfully. "When he was telling me about his dog, I never thought he was lying about any of it. I believed everything he said about Pride being a great dog, pillar of the breed, all that. And how he was so brokenhearted when the dog died. He didn't seem like he was lying, did he, Dick?"

March smiled and shook her head. "He wasn't lying.

118

That's the way he remembers it. He has to remember it that way or he wouldn't be able to stand it."

A silent signal passed between her and Dan, and together they stood up and said good night. Back toward their Winnebago they walked, a tall, soft, gentle man and a sturdy woman who resembled Kathryn Gorsuch more than she knew.

HILLEL TORAH DAY SCHOOL